CRAZY FOR YOU

MADDIE JAMES

Zebra Books
Kensington Publishing Corp.

http://www.zebrabooks.com

ZEBRA BOOKS are published by

Kensington Publishing Corp.
850 Third Avenue
New York, NY 10022

Copyright © 1999 by Kim Whalen

All rights reserved. No part of this book may be reproduced in any form or by any means without the prior written consent of the Publisher, excepting brief quotes used in reviews.

If you purchased this book without a cover you should be aware that this book is stolen property. It was reported as "unsold and destroyed" to the Publisher and neither the Author nor the Publisher has received any payment for this "stripped book."

Zebra and the Z logo Reg. U.S. Pat. & TM Off.

First Printing: October, 1999
10 9 8 7 6 5 4 3 2 1

Printed in the United States of America

BOOK YOUR PLACE ON OUR WEBSITE AND MAKE THE READING CONNECTION!

We've created a customized website just for our very special readers, where you can get the inside scoop on everything that's going on with Zebra, Pinnacle and Kensington books.

When you come online, you'll have the exciting opportunity to:

- View covers of upcoming books
- Read sample chapters
- Learn about our future publishing schedule (listed by publication month *and author*)
- Find out when your favorite authors will be visiting a city near you
- Search for and order backlist books from our online catalog
- Check out author bios and background information
- Send e-mail to your favorite authors
- Meet the Kensington staff online
- Join us in weekly chats with authors, readers and other guests
- Get writing guidelines
- AND MUCH MORE!

**Visit our website at
http://www.zebrabooks.com**

Coming October 1999 From Bouquet Romances

#17 Somewhere In The Night by Marcia Evanick
__(0-8217-6373-3, $3.99) When Detective Chad Barnett finds Bridget McKenzie trembling at his door, the devastating memories of the case they worked on together five years ago come rushing back. While he can't deny the beautiful clairvoyant's plea for help, he knows he must resist the tender feelings she stirs in his heart.

#18 Unguarded Hearts by Lynda Sue Cooper
__(0-8217-6374-1, $3.99) Pro-basketball coach Mitch Halloran would have sent the gorgeous blonde bodyguard packing, but death threats were no joke—and Nina Wild didn't take "no" for an answer. But when Nina becomes the target of his stalker, he realizes she's the one woman in the world he isn't willing to lose.

#19 And Then Came You by Connie Keenan
__(0-8217-6375-X, $3.99) When attorney Cole Jaeger returns to Montana to sell the ranch he inherited from his uncle, he discovers one big problem—feisty beauty Sarah Keller, who not only lives at the ranch, but has the crazy notion that he's a rugged cowboy with a love of country life and a heart of gold.

#20 Perfect Fit by Lynda Simmons
__(0-8217-6376-8, $3.99) Wedding gown designer Rachel Banks creates dresses brides can only dream of, even if her own dreams have nothing to do with matrimony. But when blue-eyed charmer Mark Robison shows up at his sister's final fitting, sparks fly between the two.

Call toll free **1-888-345-BOOK** to order by phone or use this coupon to order by mail.
Name_____
Address_____
City_____ State _____Zip _____
Please send me the books I have checked above.
I am enclosing $_____
Plus postage and handling $_____
Sales tax (where applicable) $_____
Total amount enclosd $_____
*Add $2.50 for the first book and $.50 for each additional book.
Send check or Money order (no cash or CODs) to:
Kensington Publishing Corp., 850 Third Avenue, New York, NY 10022
Prices and Numbers subject to change without notice. Valid only in the U.S.
All Books will be available 10/1/99. All orders subject to availability.
Check out our web site at **www.kensingtonbooks.com**

FEB 2000

Dear Readers,

One of the nicest things about the Bouquet line is the burgeoning of a multitude of brand-new blossoms we're cultivating in our newly seeded garden of love. Four of them have burst into bloom this month, just in time for a fabulous fall flowering.

Take a woman hiding, under an assumed name, in a small Maine town, and a man hiding from life itself; add the rescue of a couple of cute kids, and you have Wendy Morgan's debut romance, **Loving Max.**

Grab a bikini and head for the tropics. Roast beef meets tofu when flower child Tasha and button-down salesman Andrew Powell III meet at a singles resort in Maddie James's rollicking romance, **Crazy For You.** Then, in Michaila Callan's **Love Me Tender**, travel to small-town Texas, where Eden Karr employs a handsome carpenter to redesign her boutique . . . and gets a new design for living and loving as well! Finally, fly to faraway, fantastical Caldonia, where New York magazine editor Nicole is hired to find a queen for handsome Prince Rand—before the end of the year—in **The Prince's Bride** by Tracy Cozzens. Will his coach turn into a pumpkin before her mission is acomplished . . . or will love find a way?

Speaking of pumpkins, we'll be back next month with four splendid new Bouquet romances—in brilliant fall colors. Look for us!

The Editors

CRAZY FOR HER

"Isn't this wonderful?" Tasha said, finally leaning back on the warm dock. After all that talk, she and Andrew had cleared the obstacles of their past and their present. All that remained were the obstacles of the future. They might not be so easy to break down, but that could wait until the next long talk. . . .

"Finally, we're free," she whispered, arching her neck to pay homage to the sun. "We've shed the trappings of our society. We're at one with nature. I never dreamed I could feel so . . ."

Andrew had had just about all he could stand. Didn't she realize she was driving him crazy? Reaching over, he grasped her chin in his hand and dipped his head to hers. As he pulled her closer to him, her eyes flew open in surprise. But before he would allow her to say a word, he crushed his lips down on hers.

"Don't . . . you . . . ever . . . shut . . . up?" he growled between nibbles and kisses. The gentle rolling of the dock rocked them closer to each other. Desire, deep and apparent to them both, coursed through him to her, heating their flesh in every place their skin touched. Which was just about everywhere. . . .

PROLOGUE

I can't do it.

Tasha Smith glanced to her right at Mark Tyler. His black suit fit nicely. The crisp white shirt was starched to perfection; his gray striped tie was tucked neatly between his lapels. Every hair was combed into place with precision. He was handsome, with chiseled features and a body that wouldn't quit. Of course, she'd thought that since they were children. She was deeply fond of him, and he loved her. But as he stared straight ahead, a slight smile on his lips, listening intently to the minister's words, she couldn't help the thought that had run through her head for weeks now.

Longer, if she really cared to admit it.

I can't go through with this.

Slowly, she angled her gaze toward the minister. His lips were moving but her brain didn't comprehend a single spoken word. Glancing lower, she caught sight of the dress she'd purchased in Denver months ago. The gauzy, cream-colored fabric flowed from high under her breasts, the empire style accentuating her slim waist. The hemline was long and swirled around her ankles. Blades of grass poked at her feet between the straps of her tan sandals. All around her, the Rocky Mountains called, beckoning her thoughts away from what was going on around her.

Her mother's garden was a beautiful setting for a wedding, the floral essence romantic against the crisp clean mountain air. They had planned this for so long. Too long, actually—it always seemed they were putting it off. . . .

A breeze blew playfully through her long brown hair, and Tasha silently wished she could sail away on that breeze to some distant, mythical place where she wouldn't be troubled by the right, or the wrong, thing to do.

Her eyes opened wide at that revelation, which hit like a fist of ice into her belly. Oh, God. She was making a terrible mistake.

I really can't do this.

With a quick glance at Mark, she let her hand drop from his grasp. The other arm fell and the bouquet she was carrying lay loose in her hand.

Mark glanced at her, then back to the minister.

"So if there is anyone here with just reason as to why these two young people should not be joined in holy matrimony today, let them come forward now, or forever hold their peace."

Tasha let her wedding bouquet fall completely to the ground.

Silence.

Turning her gaze toward Mark, she heaved a deep sigh and met his questioning stare.

"I'm so sorry," she whispered.

CRAZY FOR YOU 7

Turning, she ran blindly up the aisle through the garden.

"You have to talk to him."
"I can't."
"You must, Tasha. You've just broken that young man's heart. You have to say something to him."

Tasha lifted her gaze from the wet tissues in her lap to her mother's unhappy but sympathetic face. Her mother was right, she should talk to Mark. But right now, she couldn't bear to do it. Right now, she could barely stand herself.

Outside the window of what had been her bedroom at her parents' house, a small bird chirped happily. Normally, she would have sat as still as possible and listened to the melodic song, but right now, even that didn't cheer her. She'd hurt Mark so badly.

"He'll never forgive me, Mama." She dabbed at her eyes. "And I don't blame him. He's my best friend. I've loved him since I was a child. I'm just not *in* love with him, and I've led him on for way too long, Mama. I should have told him months ago. I should have been straight with him."

Nodding, her mother handed her the box of tissues. "Yes, you should have, but you weren't. Don't make the same mistake twice. Talk to the man, Tasha."

Tasha glanced away and stared out the window.

The bird was gone now. There was no more happy chirping.

She shook her head. "No. I can't. Not now."

ONE

"You should get away from here for a while."

Tasha looked at her mother and tossed her a sarcastic smile. "Oh, yeah? And who do you propose should run the shop while I'm gone?"

"Me! Who else?" Her mother grinned broadly.

Tasha laughed. "You? I can barely get you to work twenty hours a week! And where would I go?"

"Oh, there are places."

Just like her mother, she thought, to be vague and mysterious and smiling like a Cheshire cat all the while.

It had been exactly one month since Tasha left Mark at the altar. She'd been avoiding him for as long, trying to get her head together, but it was hard. He called the shop every day or so, just to see how she was doing, but she'd asked her mother to fend off his calls. It was difficult enough to speak to him, not to mention facing everyone else in town. Living in Pinebow Springs, Colorado, where everyone knew everyone else—and their business—made things difficult enough. Sure, it was possible she needed to get away for a while, but this little shop was her livelihood and—

"What did you say, Moontasha?"

Surprised, she glanced back to her mother. "Did I say something?"

"You were muttering."

"I was?"

"Um-hmm . . . you were."

Tasha waved her mother off, barely throwing her a glance. Should she take some time off? This thing with Mark was a bit unnerving. She didn't have the money to go anywhere just now. Maybe in the spring . . .

But could her mother *really* handle taking over the shop for a week? Violet usually worked only part time. The remainder of her week she practiced homeopathy.

The bell over the door chimed and Tasha looked up. Her mother, of course, had disappeared. She'd just have to think about this later.

Running a hand through her waist-length hair, Tasha approached her customer. Her bare feet padded across the smooth plank floor as she straightened the loose, ankle-length, cotton dress draped around her tall, thin body. Tucking a stray strand of hair behind her right ear, she approached the woman from the side.

"Help you find anything?" Tasha offered with a smile.

"Tomatoes," the woman answered bluntly, fingering a plump ripe one, then turning a wary eye on Tasha. "I want to know about your tomatoes. Where are they grown?"

CRAZY FOR YOU 11

Tasha cleared her throat. Her customers sure were picky, always wanting to know this and that about her fruits and vegetables. Well, she couldn't blame them. In this day and age not much you came by was grown naturally. She was half afraid to eat anything if she didn't know where or how it was grown.

Her own interest in the subject and her study of herbs and essential oils made this a perfect business for her. Her shop, *Naturally*, catered to individuals who wanted only the purest fruits, vegetables, and herbs they could buy. On the side, Tasha had even begun studying medicinal home remedies using herbs and oils. Recently she'd become quite taken with the practice of aromatherapy. There was so much to share with her customers, and most of them were quite interested.

"The Tom Jones farm over in the next county." Tasha placed the back of her hand over her mouth and yawned. "Those on the left were hydroponically grown in a hothouse. No pesticides. The ones on the right were grown in just plain old dirt. Compost and manure for fertilization, and of course the proper added nutrients—to the soil, that is," she returned. "How many can I get you?"

The woman assessed her. Tasha was known for her candid manner, and it had paid off in her business. Her customers wanted to know what was what and she gave it to them up front. Word of mouth brought her most of her business. She was quite proud of her success.

"I'll take about three pounds of those on the right. No, better make it four. I'm making marinara sauce." She snapped her fingers. "Do you have any fresh basil?"

"On the back wall," Tasha returned. "You want to pick out your tomatoes?"

The customer nodded as though the idea were her own, reached for a brown paper bag on the shelf above the tomatoes, and began gingerly to lay several in the bottom.

"Bring them over when you're ready and I'll weigh them," Tasha said as she headed back to the counter. "Got some nice corn over there, too. Sweet as sugar. Came from the Sagesar place over by the river. Good bottom land. Might want to check it out."

The woman nodded and turned away. Tasha returned to the counter, suddenly lost in thought again. Maybe she should try to get away. She'd drunk so much valerian tea the past month her nerves should be calm and darned near sedated, but they weren't.

Perhaps her mother was right; she did need to get away, and she'd managed to save a little money. It was just like her mother to plant seeds in her head. Violet knew her all too well. The idea tantalized her more with each passing moment.

Maybe she'd find one of those New Age spas. Yes, that's it. She could hike every day and commune with nature. Maybe she'd take up meditating again, even brush up on her yoga. She'd been far too stressed lately with the wedding plans, the embarrassment of dumping Mark as she had, and then Mark's being so upset . . .

Oh, well. That was all over. It was time to get back on track and in tune with her life. Deep in her heart she knew she and Mark never should have attempted marriage. They were too good friends to destroy that relationship. Soon he would come to see that, she hoped. She just had to put his pain out of her mind for a while.

Glancing up, she watched the woman drift across the room to set the bag of tomatoes on the counter, then leave them to stroll toward the sweet corn. Tasha stretched her arms out in front of her. She rolled the diamond and sapphire ring she wore on her right hand back upright. It caught just a glimmer of sunlight through the window and Tasha smiled. Her one indulgence: jewelry, and expensive jewelry at that. Her mother chastised her for it daily.

Cupping her chin in her hands while perching her elbows on the counter, Tasha glanced around the cozy shop. This was her life. She knew it now, even though it had taken her several years to realize.

She still hadn't totally embraced the hippie lifestyle of her parents, but there was no doubt she had a lot of it in her. After fighting it—and them—for several years, she'd finally given in and decided she was the offspring of hippie baby boomers who'd risked making love, not war, and raised a flower child without benefit of matrimony, a child who'd grown up confused about living in a material world of which she'd never felt a part. Once she'd figured all that out, she realized she was pretty special—one of a kind. So she'd gone with it and was perfectly happy.

Until recently. Recently she'd felt so . . . unsettled. So . . . scattered.

Sighing, she savored the silence of the room. Only the soft whir of the old paddle fan in the center of the ceiling broke the quiet. She liked it that way. She didn't necessarily bring in much money, but she was successful enough and she liked the calm her livelihood brought to her each day. No way would she be caught in the traditional nine-to-five stress trap. Vegetables were safe and soothing. They couldn't make sexist remarks or talk back. And, boy, was she ever glad. She'd talked to a zillion of them.

"Moontasha Begonia!" Violet peeked out at her from between the curtains covering the opening to the back room. Tasha turned to her mother. "Don't you ever do anything but daydream, girl? How you run this business I'll never know. Delivery truck out back!"

Tasha stood upright, slipped her feet into her clogs, and bent to scratch at her ankle—the one with the small rose tattoo right above it. "Oh, okay. Can you get this customer?"

Her mother nodded and stepped up behind the counter as Tasha went out the back door.

Andrew Jacob Powell III hadn't taken a vacation in over ten years, and he didn't want to take one now. It didn't matter what anyone said.

Unless, of course, that anyone was his boss.

He glanced around the room at his associates. A light haze of smoke from Doug Johnston's cigar hung over the conference table. The whole world was going smokeless. Why hadn't Hayward and Pendleton caught on yet? Then he peered across the table to his immediate supervisor, Martin Mayes, whose eyes were trained on him.

Andrew swallowed, then repeated his conviction. "Really, sir. The incentive program has merit, especially for new sales associates. However, as a veteran of the firm, I feel it would be wrong of me to accept—"

Mayes rose. "Nonsense!"

Andrew straightened in the padded leather seat and again glanced around the conference room. All eyes were on him.

Mayes continued, "Doug and Brett worked for a month or more on this incentive program, and with outstanding results. Sales are up, and we have you to thank."

Mayes stepped slowly and determinedly around the room toward Andrew. Andrew's palms grew damp. Involuntarily, his hand went to his neck and he loosened his tie. How he hated these meetings. Mayes stepped behind him and put his hands on Andrew's shoulders. Andrew tried hard not to tense his shoulder muscles.

"You did a fantastic job this quarter, Powell."

"Actually my figures were down a bit, sir," Andrew interjected.

Mayes patted his shoulder and continued, "But still above any of the other associates', Andrew.

Well above. Of course, consistency is important, and you are always that—consistent. Always on the money. I think it most appropriate that our first incentive award be presented to you."

Quickly, his hands left Andrew's shoulders and he stepped away. "Get with Doug, Andrew. He's worked out all the details. And remember, it's a paid vacation, in addition to your regular accumulated days. May do you some good. Work the kinks out at that resort. Your shoulders are tied up in knots."

Andrew's gaze fell to the polished table.

"Yes, Andrew," Doug Johnston chuckled. "You must go."

Warily, Andrew slid his gaze from Doug to Mayes as the latter sat again and picked up a piece of paper, dismissing the previous conversation. "Now, what's next on the agenda?"

Andrew glanced across the table to Doug again, knowing full well there was more here than met the eye. The competition around this table was tremendous. Why would Doug be so insistent about this trip? He'd been trying to beat Andrew's figures for three years now. Why would he want a rival to get this incentive?

Narrowing his gaze, Andrew deepened his thought on that subject while he eyed his coworker. Was Doug that desperate to get him away from the office for a week? And why?

Tasha checked her watch, flipped her backpack more securely over her shoulder, and picked up speed as she ran through the crowded airport. Flight 224J was set to take off in five minutes for Dallas and she was halfway across the Denver airport, running to beat the band, before the last call to board.

Just as the flight attendant prepared to close the door, Tasha leaped toward her, ticket and boarding pass in hand. She shoved them at the woman.

"This is my flight," she gasped, mentally chastising herself for that second cup of chamomile tea this morning, the one that made her so warm and cozy she'd fallen asleep on the couch until her mother called.

"Okay," the attendant responded. She tore the stub off the ticket and handed the rest back. "Hurry."

Tasha did, loping down the ramp toward the 737's open door, her backpack heavy on her right shoulder, a small carry-on in her left hand. Good thing she'd decided to travel light and not check her luggage, she thought. Her hiking boots weighed on her feet, though, and she felt as if she were lumbering. But she made it, bursting through the door and startling the flight attendant, who glanced quickly at her ticket and pointed down the aisle.

"We're nearly ready for takeoff. A few people have changed seats. Just sit wherever you want. There's a nice window seat near the front. It's yours if you want it."

Since Tasha's ticket was clearly marked "coach," she thought for once she'd take advantage of what was handed to her and accept the business-class seat. "Cool," she responded as she made her way down the aisle.

She spotted the lone seat immediately, puzzled as to why anyone would leave the window seat open and choose the aisle. She always wanted the window. Not that she was a world traveler or anything. It was just that when she flew, she'd always loved to look out over the postage-stamp view below.

As she neared the seat, she spotted the man sitting on the aisle. The word stuffy immediately came to mind. He was dressed in a tie, starched white shirt, and suit pants. Wire-rimmed glasses perched low across his nose. His blond hair was conservatively cut. Definitely a nine-to-fiver, she decided. Maybe a nine-to-niner or worse. It was a shame. He was probably not much older than she was. She'd always likened a businessman like that to an ugly duckling—a free spirit trapped inside a suit, secretly dying to get out.

A laptop was open on top of his briefcase; his fingers flew across the keyboard. She had to wonder about a man who couldn't stop thinking about business long enough to relax during a brief layover. To her way of thinking, something was definitely wrong with that scenario. Oh, well, it was none of her business. *Perhaps he'll get off in Dallas,* she thought. Even that was a three-hour flight.

Tasha stopped beside his seat, glanced overhead, then dropped her carry-on bag to the floor. She grazed her fingers under the compartment

CRAZY FOR YOU   19

above his head to find the latch so she could stow her backpack inside. At that point, the flight attendant came over the speaker to remind everyone to buckle up. Tasha glanced at the attendant and caught her stern gaze as her hand tripped the switch. Mr. Laptop was oblivious to everything as the compartment door swung vigorously upward. Then, quite suddenly, a blanket, a small makeup bag, and two pillows rained down on him.

Tasha yelped. The flight attendant stopped talking. Mr. Laptop simply stared straight ahead, his fingers frozen over the keyboard. A woman three seats back shouted, "That's my bag!"

Finally, Tasha moved. "Oh, I'm so sorry. Here, let me get that."

Dropping her backpack to the floor with her carry-on, Tasha grabbed one of the pillows and tossed it back up above. The flight attendant droned on again in the background and Tasha nervously glanced around at the other passengers. They weren't paying a bit of attention to her or the flight attendant. She still hadn't looked Mr. Laptop in the face. Grabbing another pillow, she tossed it upward as well.

By now the owner of the makeup bag had come forward. The man in the aisle seat removed the blanket from his lap and handed it to her, still not looking up. But when Tasha reached for the handle of the makeup bag and lifted it, the latch popped. The entire contents spilled into his lap. Tasha gasped. Mr. Laptop looked at her then— dead on—and stared quite sternly into her face.

"Are you finished?" he finally asked.

Tasha grinned nervously. "Uh . . . well, I think so." Then she looked down and saw the sticky mass of dark brown liquid makeup oozing into the cracks around the keys of the laptop. "Ohmigosh!"

She picked up the makeup bottle, capped it, and thrust it at the woman behind her. Then she snatched eyeliner and lipstick and brushes and makeup remover from his lap and the computer and tossed them into the bag, wondering all the while why any woman would slather this stuff all over her face. When a tube of mascara slid between his legs, she started to reach for it, too, then jerked her hand back. Her wide-eyed gaze went to his face; his gaze met hers.

Blue eyes. Oh, God. Bluer than a clear Rocky Mountain afternoon.

Tasha swallowed, her mouth gone suddenly dry, then pointed to the mascara. "You get that one," she said, her gaze still locked with his. He turned his attention to his lap.

"Ahem, yes. I think I'll do that."

After he'd retrieved the elusive mascara and popped it into the bag, Tasha snapped the clasp and shoved the bag toward the woman, then searched for something to wipe the makeup from the computer. The attendant came up behind her.

"Miss, you must take your seat now," she said firmly.

"But I . . ." Tasha saw the exasperation in her eyes. She nodded. "I'll take my seat now."

First, she hoisted her heavy backpack up over the man and into the compartment, crowding into him slightly. Then she grabbed her carry-on and tossed it onto the floor in front of her seat. When she tried to ease past his knees, he rose a bit out of his seat, still clutching the makeup-covered computer, to let her pass. Just as she was clear, her foot caught on the strap of her carry-on and she tripped into her seat, catching his right arm in the process and dragging him to the right with her. He scrambled back up and into his own seat.

His glasses sat a little cockeyed on his face, but he quickly righted them.

Tasha sighed and leaned back against the seat. Her head fell for a second against the headrest and she momentarily closed her eyes. She was exhausted. This vacation her mother had given her—bless her kind soul—was supposed to relax her, wasn't it? My goodness! So far she'd overslept, almost missed her flight, and ruined a man's laptop all in the same day!

This was not relaxing.

Yes, Violet had surprised her all right. The day after she'd suggested Tasha get away from Pinebow Springs for a while, she'd shown up with Club Regale Resort reservations and airline tickets in hand. A gift, she'd said. By that time Tasha was thoroughly convinced she did need to get away and she'd be grateful to her mother forever for providing her the opportunity.

Abruptly recalling the gummed-up laptop, she jerked her gaze back to the man's computer and reached for her bag. "I think I've got something in here to clean that up with," she half muttered. After finding some tissues, she reached for the computer. Startled when he pulled it back onto his lap, she met his gaze. "Let me clean it off for you."

"No, thank you. I'll have it looked at professionally." He popped the lid of the computer shut.

She stopped his hands with hers. "Just let me get the big stuff off. It will dry on there and everything."

Tasha watched as his gaze fell to her hand for a moment. Then he removed his hand from beneath hers, finished fastening the computer back together, and set both it and his briefcase at his feet. He looked at her in defiance. "Put on your seat belt."

Surprised, Tasha stared back at him. "What?"

"You're a walking disaster. The way things are going, this plane will crash. Put on your seat belt," he returned matter-of-factly. Then he reached down to fasten his with a loud snap, his gaze still connected with hers.

Tasha did as she was told, breaking the connection with his eyes. The seat belt sign was on anyway, she reasoned. She wasn't doing it because he'd ordered her. She glanced at him once more. He'd put his head back against the headrest and his eyes were closed, his fingers laced together over his abdomen. She let her gaze drift slowly over him from head to knee—and was almost afraid to admit she liked what she saw. He was too damned attractive for her own good. Who would have thought it? A man in a suit. He appeared to be asleep, but Tasha knew better. He was simply avoiding her.

Her heart was beating rapidly, and it wasn't from exhaustion. It was sexual energy, pure and simple. The vibes were good, as her mother would say. Even for a businessman.

Turning, she forced herself to look out the window and dismiss him as he had her. The airport raced rapidly by and the plane nosed higher into the air.

Why was it, Andrew thought to himself as the plane rumbled, lifted, and became airborne, he always found himself seated next to a lunatic? It never failed. In movies, at restaurants, and always on airplanes, crazy people searched him out to sit next to him as if he were a nut magnet.

And, boy, was she something. He'd tried not to look at her as she'd bumbled down the aisle toward him. He'd heard the flight attendant point out the seat next to his and he'd cringed. He hated being closed in. That's why he'd wanted the aisle and had been relieved when he'd realized, as the plane was filling, that the seat beside his might be empty. Since he was slightly claustrophobic, the aisle and an empty seat next to him always helped somewhat. But now here she was, all five feet, ten inches or more of her, he guessed. Mostly legs, he thought as he remembered her standing next to him dressed in that ridiculous getup: khaki shorts, hiking boots and thick woolen socks, a Grateful Dead T-shirt, obviously without the proper underwear beneath, a bandanna around her neck, and an Oakland A's baseball cap with a long brunette ponytail pulled through it. Whatever happened to femininity?

Legs. Andrew opened his eyes slightly and risked a glance to his right. She was staring out the window; he glanced lower. A lot of leg, actually. She crossed one over the other and he groaned inwardly. He tried to ignore the tightening in his groin and clamped his eyes shut again. Those shorts did little to cover what seemed to be miles and miles of nothing but tan, smooth, firm, luscious—and, yes, despite her ridiculous attire, very feminine—legs.

Andrew wrinkled his brow as he tried to remember the last time he'd had legs like that wrapped around him.

Never, he concluded. He'd never had legs like that wrapped around him. Too bad she was a nut. Thank God the flight was only three hours. He'd be rid of her in Dallas.

TWO

Tasha watched their descent into Dallas-Fort Worth from her window. After three hours of trying not to look at him, she finally risked a glance his way. As the plane touched down, he jolted slightly in his seat and sat upright. Perhaps he really had slept the whole time, Tasha thought. She watched as he removed his glasses, laid them in his lap, then rubbed his eyes as if trying to massage away a headache.

Definitely not a bad looking specimen, she mused. If only she could get him out of that suit of armor and into some comfortable clothing. He covered those sexy eyes of his with his glasses and then reached to the floor to retrieve his things. The ring finger of his left hand was conspicuously bare. Not that that meant anything in this day and age—her own parents were proof of that— but perhaps . . .

"I'd like to pay for any damages to your computer," Tasha blurted out, interrupting her own thoughts.

He looked at her as if he'd forgotten she was there. "No, it's all right. It belongs to the company. They have insurance, I'm sure."

Tasha let her gaze rest on the cool blue of his eyes underneath thick dark blond eyebrows. "Well, if you're sure. I can give you my address and you can contact me if—"

He waved his hand in the air. "No, we'll take care of it." He turned away from her.

The plane taxied slowly and passengers ignored the command to remain seated until they'd fully stopped. Tasha simply sat, and so did he. Finally, he looked at her. "I can let you out to get your things now."

Tasha shook her head. "I'm going on to the next stop. You go ahead."

His eyes widened, and he continued to stare at her. "I'm . . . I'm going on also." His Adam's apple bobbed up and down as he swallowed hard. "Miami?"

Tasha nodded. "Uh-huh. Miami."

Clearing his throat, he stared past her out the window. "Ah. Me, too."

"Visiting family?" she queried.

He jerked his gaze back to her, then away again quickly. "Uh, no. Business," he said. "You?"

Tasha watched him fiddle nervously with his tie and wondered why he'd just lied to her. She could tell. She could always tell when people lied to her. "Vacation."

He nodded, then faced back to the front of the plane. It was a short layover to pick up a few passengers so they were not permitted to deplane. Finally, the attendant addressed them again to alert them of their flight status and takeoff. The seat belt sign went back on.

"You have a name?" Tasha finally asked, tired of the obligatory banter.

"Excuse me?"

"Name," she replied. "Do you have one?"

He nodded, then held out his hand. For a split second, Tasha thought she might have detected a hint of a grin. "Ah, yes. Andrew Jacob Powell III."

She should have guessed.

Tasha took his warm hand into hers, feeling the surge as their flesh connected. He gripped tighter and Tasha returned the clasp. "I'm Tasha," she whispered, still feeling the power pulsing between them. "Tasha Smith."

Then quickly, as if her hand were burning his, he let it go and pulled away. The plane jolted forward, taxiing toward the runway. Tasha felt the plane's vibrations all around her—at least she thought they were the plane's vibrations. Then, once again, they were airborne.

Reaching above the seat, Tasha pulled her backpack down to her side as she was jostled by other passengers threading through the aisle. Turning toward the front of the plane, she caught just a glimpse of the back of Andrew Jacob Powell III's blond head as he exited to his left.

Puzzled, Tasha thoughtfully followed the crowd out of the plane, through the ramp, and into the Miami airport. Andrew Powell had jumped like a horse out of a gate as soon as the plane rolled to a stop. Before she'd even had a chance to say so long, he'd left her. *What a strange man,* she thought. *Probably anal retentive.* Couldn't he have at least said something to her? Have a nice day? Enjoy your vacation? I like your legs?

Oh, yes, he definitely liked her legs. He hadn't stared at them for the past four hours for his health. He'd tried to make her *think* he was asleep, but he hadn't been. A girl could tell.

Her eyes searched the crowd as they collectively followed the signs to the baggage claim area. Although she had no baggage to claim, she looked for information about her connecting flight into Montego Bay. Still, her eyes carefully darted back and forth over the crowd as she moved along. She wasn't really looking for him. She was simply . . . looking.

Was she? Was she looking for a man? Jeez . . . she always had a man in her life, didn't she? She'd just ended this thing with Mark. Why was she even interested in pursuing a man? It was not the right time to do that. But there was something about Andrew Jacob Powell. . . .

Poor Mark. He'd been her friend forever. How could she have dismissed him so quickly?

Truth be told, Tasha, she told herself, *there was nothing quick about it.* She'd contemplated the breakup for way too long before she'd acted, and she hadn't dismissed him from her life. She still wanted him—for her best friend, not her husband and lover.

Remember, girl, that's what this trip is all about—a week to get your head together so you can face Mark and tell him you love him only for the lifelong friend he is so both of you can get on with your lives.

It wasn't going to be easy facing Mark again, but she had to do it and she desperately needed this week to gather her courage.

A crowd had gathered at the baggage area, ready to claim their luggage and be gone, but Tasha kept walking, finally finding the information about her connecting flight, and began the search for her gate.

A few minutes later, she stepped out into the bright Miami sunshine and watched the small commuter aircraft which was supposed to take her to Jamaica begin a slow taxi toward the runway.

Without her.

With a thorough and contented sigh, Andrew sank back into his seat. Closing his eyes, he let his head drift to one side as he contemplated the past few hours.

He was glad to be off the larger aircraft, away from the crowds, and on the smaller, more personal plane. Even though it was barely more than puddle jumper, he felt a little less harried without so many people around. In fact, only the two-man crew up front and three other passengers were aboard. Thankfully, he didn't see any potential nuts around to bother him.

Even more, he was glad to be nearly finished with this final leg of the trip. Two days ago he had dreaded this so-called vacation. Now he was looking forward to it in an odd sort of way.

He was looking forward to a few hours of solitude—a nice clean hotel room, a nice hot shower, and a nice long nap. Later he'd find something to eat and a little nightlife. Until then, he wanted nothing but pure solitude.

His day so far had been nothing but chaos.

Shaking his head, he tried to rid himself of any lingering thoughts of the crazy brunette he'd shared the first three-fourths of his trip with. She was the opposite of any woman he'd ever dated, but there was something damned appealing about her, something he couldn't quite put his finger on.

Of course, she was also nuttier than a fruitcake.

Andrew opened his eyes again and watched the Miami airport slowly roll by. Quite by accident, he realized there was a smile on his face.

Reaching up, he rubbed his hand over his mouth, as though he could erase that smile altogether. Thing was, the smile went deeper than the surface. It was inside him, as well.

No! he thought. There was absolutely nothing about that woman that was appealing to him! Not a damned thing. She was aggravating, annoying, and downright . . . earthy.

Not his type, definitely not his type.

Crazy. Yeah, she was crazy, and so was he if he sat here thinking any more about her—and smiling, to boot.

It was a moot point, anyway, because it would

have to be one damned weird coincidence if he ever ran into her again.

Andrew jerked forward in his seat as the small plane lurched to a sudden stop. There appeared to be some commotion outside, some sort of skirmish. The pilot was arguing with someone over the radio. His voice rose, but Andrew couldn't make out exactly what he was saying.

Something about a woman, a late arrival who'd missed her flight.

The door swung open. Into the plane lumbered one harried and out-of-breath Tasha Smith.

She plopped into the seat beside him, turned, and smiled broadly. He knew his eyes were rounder than silver dollars.

"Well, what a coincidence," she remarked. "Isn't this just . . . weird?"

One corner of her mouth drew up into a smirk.

Andrew groaned and tried not to smile.

"So from the literature I have here about Eden II, the Club Regale Resort where we're both staying, it says when we get to the airport in Montego Bay, we can take the bus. There are car rentals, but I understand it's very expensive. Of course, it is a two-hour trip by bus. If you'd prefer to rent a car, since we're going to the same place maybe we could split the difference and make it a little more affordable for each of us. Then we'd have a car while we're at the resort in case either of us wants to—"

"Stop."

"Excuse me?"

"I said *stop*."

Tasha turned and looked at Andrew, one eyebrow arched. "Did you want to say something?"

He couldn't believe his ears. "Yes, I would like to say something. Is that all right?"

She tossed him an odd look. "Well, yes. Of course it's all right. What would you like to say?"

As he looked into her eyes and an amusing expression crept across her face, he couldn't think of what he wanted to say. For the life of him, at that moment Andrew couldn't think of a word. He'd listened to her jabber on for nearly an hour. There was no way he could get a word in edgewise. Once she'd found out they were heading to the same resort, it was all downhill.

Now he was speechless.

Hell, she practically had their entire week planned out.

Andrew snorted. By the end of the week, she'd be making wedding plans if he didn't stop things right this—

"You were going to say?"

Andrew jerked his gaze back up to her face. Somehow, he'd been staring at her legs again.

"I was saying—"

The plane jostled and Andrew felt himself being tossed to his right, closer to Tasha. Quickly, he righted himself. "I was saying I'm not taking the bus. I have a rental. But *you*, you will be taking the bus. You *need* to take the bus. You and I will not be sharing—"

Tasha looked past him, leaning toward his window. "Oh, look! We're descending. There's the island! Can't you just imagine? Some little guy down there is yelling, 'da plane! da plane!' Can't you just hear him? I can't believe we're almost there. Isn't this exciting?"

Andrew inhaled deeply and rubbed a hand over his face. Woodsy perfume filled his nostrils and masses of long brunette hair filled his vision. He wanted her gone. Now, before it was too damned—

She turned and looked directly into his eyes. "It's going to be a great week, you know." Then she smiled—big, warm, and way, way too temptingly.

Late. Before it was too damned late.

Andrew shifted in his seat and she sat back in hers. He could feel the plane descending. Or was that something landing with a thud in the pit of his stomach? Something . . . undefinable.

"You were saying?" she began again.

Andrew shook his head. "Nothing. It was nothing."

Grinning, Tasha sat back in her seat and waited for the plane to land. Andrew waited, too. For what, he still wasn't quite sure.

With the keys to his rented Miata jangling from his hand, Andrew nervously crossed the pavement toward the rows of rental cars. He'd somehow managed to give Tasha the slip at the gate. It wasn't intentional; it had just happened. If the truth be known, he had glanced around a couple of times trying to locate her, but she was nowhere to be found, and then there was all that commotion at customs. He thought he'd seen the back of her head as he was leaving the baggage area, but he'd moved quickly to the car rental desk to get on his way.

It didn't matter. She was gone.

All the better, he thought. He had better things to do than be pestered by one Tasha Smith the remainder of the week.

As he approached the small rental lot, he thought Doug Johnston's idea might not have been too bad. He searched for row D and car space number twelve. A Miata was what he was looking for—a little sporty red Miata. *This incentive program may indeed have merit,* he thought. The way his sales figures had been over the past two years, he might be up for this often. Andrew smiled.

Ordinarily he worked way past his hours, got up early, went to bed late. Suddenly, though, he found the thought of this vacation appealing. And surely at a place like this there would be contacts—doctors, pharmacists, hospital administrators. A working vacation. Why hadn't he thought of it before?

The sign for row D came into view, and he paced the row looking for number twelve, his gaze locked on the pavement. Nine—ten—eleven—twelve. He looked up. There was the car—and there was *Tasha* pushing a key into the door lock of his sporty red Miata.

"Whoa." He stepped up to her. "I think you've

got the wrong vehicle here." She snapped her gaze to him, pulled the key from the lock, and straightened her tall body. Andrew felt that same unwelcome thud in the pit of his stomach again as her large brown eyes met his.

"This is your car?" Her voice was as thick as honey.

"Well, yes." He glanced at the ticket attached to the keys, then thrust them toward her. "D-12. A Miata. That's mine."

She looked at her own keys, then flashed them toward him. "Don't think so, see? D-12. Says so right here. I wasn't expecting a Miata, but I'm not complaining." She reached down to the handle and lifted it. "Besides, the key fits." She opened the car, tossed her carry-on and backpack over to the passenger's side, got in and slammed the door.

Wide-eyed, Andrew stepped next to the door and pounded on the window as the ignition ground to a start. "Hey! What do you think you're doing? This is my car!"

She smiled at him. That damned, beautiful, aggravating nut smiled at him.

"I don't think so." She mouthed the words through the window, drawing them out slowly. Still smiling, she pulled the gear shift into reverse.

Andrew's blood roiled in his veins. He watched as she backed out, then jogged along beside her. "You can't do this! You're crazy!" He pounded on the window again. She continued in reverse until the car was fully backed out of the space and pointed toward the exit. After a moment of staring at one another through the tinted glass, finally she let the window down halfway.

"What is your problem?" she asked, her doe-like eyes wide and questioning. "Do you always act like this? Are you stressed? Perhaps you should try ginseng. Works wonders, you know."

My problem? Ginseng?

"*You're* crazy," he repeated. "Like I told you, a walking disaster. Get out of there so we can settle this."

Acting the innocent, she asked, "Settle what?"

"Look. Obviously there's been a mix-up."

"I don't think so," she said calmly, shaking her head.

Disbelief flooded through him. How could someone be so obstinate and rude—and at the same time so intriguingly beautiful?

Reaching for the door handle, he tipped it forward and found it locked, which only aggravated him more. "I *do* think so," he said.

"Nope." The window rolled all the way up and she revved the engine.

The Miata began rolling, picking up speed. But before it reached the exit, the car slowed to a stop. Tasha got out and faced him again.

Andrew saw her hands go to her mouth as she shouted. He jogged a few steps closer and strained to hear her above the roar of a plane engine across the way. "What a creep!" he thought he heard her say. She pointed behind him.

He looked, scanning the rows of cars for a moment. When he looked back, all he saw were the taillights of the Miata as they were swallowed into traffic.

What a creep? How dare she call me names, he thought as he backtracked through the parking lot. Pain from the stress of the afternoon raced across his forehead. *What a creep?*

Andrew scratched his head in amazement. When he stopped walking, he found himself dead in front of a four-wheel drive vehicle. *A creep? Me? Why, she doesn't even know me. If I ever get my hands on that—"*

Jeep.

His gaze landed on the lettering on the back of the vehicle. He blinked, then read the four-letter word again. A Jeep?

And then it clicked. Could she have said—

Try the Jeep?

Several minutes later, Tasha found herself thoroughly enjoying her cruise down the narrow coastal highway. The ocean roared on her left; green hills and trees bordered the road on the right. Such a pleasant drive, she thought, and Eden II beckoned. Even the name sounded decadent and relaxing. Lord knew she needed it after this afternoon. Stress? Andrew Jacob Powell III oozed it, and too much had worn off on her. But she had good old Andrew to thank for the Miata.

Downshifting, she slowed for a hill and curve and then looked out over the ocean and sighed.

She felt kind of bad, really, leaving Andrew Powell III back there in the parking lot empty-handed. That's why, on second thought, she'd told him about the Jeep. *He's intelligent enough to figure out the keys were switched,* she told herself. He'd probably go back to the desk and get another little red Miata. Could she help it if the lady behind the desk made a mistake and gave her the wrong keys?

Of course, that switch got a little nudge when the lady behind the desk had to take a phone call and turned her back. But, after all, Tasha had been taught never to look a gift horse in the mouth.

This was some nifty little gift horse.

But she shouldn't have left him standing there. Served him right, though, darting off the plane without even a fare-thee-well and giving her the slip as soon as he'd gotten through customs, the arrogant little stuck-up Nordic god. *I bet his mother still does his laundry.*

Reaching up to adjust the rearview mirror, Tasha caught sight of a vehicle closing in behind her fast. Suddenly, it swerved to the left as it neared her bumper and pulled up beside her.

Oh, damn. She hadn't expected this.

Andrew spotted the Miata ahead of him, *his* little sporty red Miata, and his insides turned to molten lava. It couldn't be.

If he had ever been angry enough to strangle someone, this was it. He had promised himself if he got one minute alone with that lunatic, he'd throttle her. He just hadn't realized it would be today. Hell, might as well get the damned thing over. He'd have murder on his hands come sundown.

He had cursed her for twenty minutes while trying the key in every damned Jeep on the lot. He'd even been accused by one of the lot attendants of trying to break into one. The man had just about called in the local authorities. Andrew had lied, something completely out of character for him, and told the man his key wouldn't fit the Jeep he was assigned. They'd searched together until they found the one the key unlocked.

And now here he was, flying down this narrow little road at a speed much faster than he should be driving, the canvas doors and roof of his so-called rental car flapping in his ears.

Pressing the accelerator to the floor, he sped up behind the vehicle, caught the outline of dark hair, a long ponytail and baseball cap, and quickly swerved left to pull up beside her.

Wide-eyed, she glanced at him, then accelerated to speed ahead down the road.

He did the same. When he caught up with her, he swung his arm toward her, motioning for her to pull over.

She smiled, then hit the accelerator again.

Andrew cursed. "I don't intend to play cat-and-mouse with you all afternoon, lady," he muttered.

As his speedometer needle steadily rose, he caught up with her again. They sped neck and neck down the narrow road. He rolled the power window down on the passenger side and yelled, "Pull over!"

She shook her head no.

"I said pull over!" He motioned for her to do so again.

She rolled her window down. "Over my dead body!"

"If you insist!"

Her eyes widened even more as she glared at him. "Go away! Leave me alone," she shouted over the whir of wheels on asphalt.

"I want my car!" Andrew shouted back, watching her ponytail billow around her neck in the wind. He'd like to put his hands around that long, slender neck.

They glared at each other.

"Pull over before we kill ourselves," he ordered again, peering over his glasses at her.

"No!" she shouted back.

Andrew shook his head and tensed his shoulder muscles. As he glanced in front of him, a large animal bolted out from his side of the road.

"Donkey!" He slammed his foot on the brake.

Tasha's startled gaze caught his. "What?"

"Look out!" But her vehicle slid ahead of his as he braked. He watched her head snap back to the road in front of her. Her brake lights flashed. The Miata skidded, leaving black marks on the road behind her.

Concentrating on keeping his own vehicle upright and on the road, Andrew was still conscious of Tasha's taillights fishtailing back and forth in front of him.

The right side of his Jeep dropped off the edge of the pavement and sank into the wet, sandy

CRAZY FOR YOU

shoulder, stopping him abruptly and jerking the Jeep entirely off the road. He cursed. And then—

Then he heard the crunch of metal against . . . against something very hard.

Dazed for a moment, Andrew shook his head until he could see clearly again. The Miata was off the side of the road ahead of him, its nose pointing into a huge boulder. *Oh, God, no.* He never intended for her to be hurt. He'd just wanted—

"Damn it, Powell. You are an idiot!"

He jumped out of the Jeep and ran up to the side of her vehicle. The window was down. Tasha was draped over the steering wheel, her back heaving up and down. Small, guttural noises were coming from her throat.

He reached out and touched her shoulder. "You okay?"

Tasha jerked her head up. "Of all the stupid, irresponsible, idiotic things . . ."

Andrew breathed a sigh of relief that she was okay, then parked his fists on his hips. "I asked if you were okay."

"Okay? *Okay?* Oh, yeah, sure, I'm okay. Are *you* okay?"

Andrew shifted his weight to his other foot and crossed his arms over his chest. "Yeah, I'm okay."

The door burst open and hit him square in the thigh, nearly knocking him off balance. Tasha jumped out, her arms flailing. "What the hell did you think you were doing back there? You could have gotten us both killed. Are you an idiot or what?"

Andrew narrowed his eyes at her. "No, actually, I think that's more your personality type, not mine. I want my car."

"Your car? You want your *car*?" She reached out and grabbed his shirt in both her hands, balling it up with her fists. Andrew felt his eyes widen. "You materialistic pig! You risked both our lives because of a stupid sports car?"

She released him with a small shove and Andrew stepped backward. His plan was—wasn't it?—that he was going to strangle *her*. What had happened?

Tasha crawled into the driver's side of the car on her hands and knees, reaching for her bags on the other side, all the while muttering about Communism and the ill wind of a fascist society. Andrew allowed his gaze to be drawn to her derriere, which poked up at him, perfectly framed in the door opening. He found himself grinning, liking the way her shorts hiked up slightly, showing the bottoms of two rounded cheeks. Then she backed out, her gear in tow, and slammed the door shut. He wiped the grin off his face as she reached in through the window to retrieve something she'd dropped on the seat.

"You want your stupid car, take your stupid car." She walked off in a huff. He let her, watching her tight little slim-hipped rear end sway in the khaki hiking shorts as she approached the Jeep, her ponytail brushing the swell of her hips. He stood there as she opened the door, reached in and grabbed his luggage and his briefcase, and tossed them onto the pavement. A passing car nearly hit them. Andrew cringed and darted forward.

"Hey! Be careful with that! It's expensive!"

"Then you'd better get it the hell off the road, hadn't you?" she shouted back.

She jumped into the Jeep and started the ignition as he stepped closer to the vehicle. She tramped on the accelerator. The Jeep didn't budge. She tried again. Sand and dirt flew up in an arc behind the Jeep as it rocked forward, then backward, then forward, then backward again. She stopped, then tried once more. More sand and gravel and dirt flew. The Jeep stayed put.

Finally, she cut the engine and glared at Andrew through the windshield. A thought occurred to him.

Frantically, he raced back toward the Miata, opened the door, and dove into the driver's seat. His fear was realized—the ignition was empty. She'd taken the damned keys.

"Need these?"

He turned. Now standing beside the Jeep, she was taunting him, the keys swaying from her fingertips, and she was smiling. The idiot was smiling.

Andrew felt as he had when his older brother used to play aggravating, teasing games with him. He didn't like it then; he didn't like it now. He was tired of this game.

"Yes, I would like the keys back, please. If you don't mind."

She smiled again.

In the next instant she threw the keys as hard

and as far as she could over the ocean side of the road, then tossed his luggage and briefcase after them.

She spared the laptop.

Andrew stood there, spellbound, and watched his things bounce off the rocks and into the ocean.

Then it started to rain.

THREE

The bus to Eden II rumbled by within fifteen minutes.

Andrew and Tasha were soaked to the skin. Tasha had to chuckle to herself. Served the guy right, she thought. Maybe now he'd get out of that awful suit and tie. Of course, she'd have to accompany him to one of the resort shops. She'd hate to see what sort of beach ensemble the guy would come up with.

Andrew was in a terrible mood and refused to flag down the bus. Tasha took matters in her own hands. The hell with the arrogant businessman. She was ready for one wild week of decadence, and she didn't care whether he came with her or not.

In fact, for a moment, she thought he was going to stand there at the side of the road and not get on the bus. At last, though, he did. He was a sight, looking like some sad, drowned puppy, clutching his laptop to his chest, wading through the sea of Club Regale party-goers to the one vacant seat on the bus.

It was far from her seat, of course, but she

didn't mind. She wasn't through with Andrew Jacob Powell III yet. Not by a long shot.

She still had six days and seven nights ahead of her.

The deep green rain forest shaded the narrow road that wound through the island jungle country like a living, breathing tunnel. Huge native wildflowers splashed color into the day, and children dashed off and onto the road, dancing in puddles and dodging vehicles and motorbikes. The rain had stopped and the sun was poking out again between the clouds. It was going to be a nice afternoon after all.

She knew they were close. She'd followed along on the map she'd been provided at the car rental desk and had located all the landmarks along the way. They were on the outskirts of Negril. The bus had made good time, it seemed, despite stopping to pick up the two of them in the rainstorm and the half hour they had lost when they'd made a pit stop at a roadside shanty so some of the guests could purchase "necessities."

She figured they should be turning a sharp curve to the left just about . . .

Now.

They had arrived.

The bus rolled between the unmarked stone pillars of the entrance and peacefulness wafted over her. As they drove slowly past palm trees, up a vine-covered incline, and around a hill, she pulled down the window beside her on the bus and drank in the essence of bliss—clean air, birds chirping, waves pounding the surf not far away.

Andrew Powell and all his idiosyncrasies were forgotten.

"Ahhh. . . . This is going to be heaven," she whispered to herself. After what she'd gone through to get here, she was ready for it.

As the bus turned another curve on the narrow unpaved road, Tasha suddenly found herself faced with a bright open area, a parking lot about half full of cars, and a magnificent structure behind it that she recognized from the pictures in the brochure as the main building for lodging.

Eden II.

A week of passion and pleasure, the brochure read, *a respite for body and soul and spirit and mind. An all-inclusive vacation package which boasts unlimited cocktails to unending nightlife to sunbathing* au naturel . . .

Did Andrew Jacob Powell III really know what he was getting into? Tasha wondered. Might be of fun to find out.

She grinned.

The bus stopped. The Regalers, as she'd begun to call the Club's party-goers, began to exit, and they were a mighty rowdy bunch!

It took her only a second to grab her backpack and her other bag, hop out, and bounce to the front of the bus to join them. No way would she miss out on the party now.

And as she exited the bus, she came face to face with the stuck-up Nordic god . . . and found herself wondering what he would look like *au naturel*.

"Hi!"

Every feature of his face fell. He hugged his laptop closer to his chest and walked briskly toward the hotel.

Tasha followed. "Imagine that. From the beginning, we were heading to the same place. Who would have thought it?"

Andrew harrumphed.

"Thought you said you were in Miami on business."

He ignored her, his gaze locked on the pavement in front of him.

"Are you in the habit of lying to people?"

Andrew stopped and turned to look at her. "Leave me alone. Go bother someone else. You're a walking time bomb, and I don't want to be around when you explode." He walked off again.

Tasha stood still for a moment. "I'm really not that bad, you know," she called after him. "You just need to loosen up."

He stopped cold in his tracks and turned slightly as if he were going to say something, thought better of it, then started once more for the hotel. Tasha took off again to reach his side.

"Look," she said, trying to keep up with his hurried strides. "I'll apologize about the car thing. It must have been this major screwup or something. It really wasn't my fault. And you have to admit you almost got us killed back there."

He just looked at her and shook his head.

They ascended the steps to the hotel.

CRAZY FOR YOU 49

"And . . . and the computer. I said I'd pay for it, although I know it was probably pretty expensive and it would take me a while, but . . ."

They reached the double glass door leading into the lobby. Andrew shuffled his laptop underneath his left arm and laid his right hand on the door handle. Tasha readjusted her backpack over her shoulder and laid her hand on his. "Maybe we could start over."

Each turned to the other. For a moment, they stood frozen. Tasha liked looking into those blue eyes. Then Andrew broke the connection, slid his hand from underneath hers, and pushed the door open, ignoring her.

He stepped into the lobby. Tasha tumbled in behind him, then stood by his side.

The room was large, with thick red carpeting and rough-hewn log walls. Plants of assorted sizes and species decorated the room. Slow-moving fans hung from huge beams stretched across the ceiling. A man stood behind a large reception desk to the left; to the right was a grouping of chairs. Across the back of the room was a wall of floor-to-ceiling windows looking out over an open area and some individual cabins. A crowded pool was visible to the left.

But something else entirely caught Tasha's eye—Andrew's too, she suspected.

The man behind the desk was nude from the waist up. That was all she could see; the desk covered him from the waist down. *My, this place must really be casual,* she thought, *to allow the workers to go shirtless.*

Shirtless?

Tasha threw a puzzled glance at Andrew. His face was pale, his gaze trained out the window. She followed his line of vision.

Squinting through the mottled glass at the distant pool, she could see the pool's occupants appeared to be swimming . . . without the proper bathing attire.

Ohmigod! Was this the *au naturel* swimming and Jacuzzi the brochure talked about right up front?

Tasha grinned. This was going to get *very* interesting very quickly.

Andrew's laptop thudded to the floor, hitting Tasha's toe. She ignored the pain and turned to him. His eyes were wide and his mouth had dropped open in astonishment. Tasha's tongue grazed her lower lip as she looked Andrew Powell up and down, wondering what he would look like without that stuffy starched white shirt.

He was doing the same to her. What *was* that look in his eyes?

Tasha hesitantly smiled. Andrew snatched up his laptop and bolted out the door.

"Wait!" She called after him as she followed him out the door. "Andrew, wait!"

When she finally caught up with him, she grasped his arm to stop him. "Look. Think about this a minute," she gasped, out of breath. "This might be fun."

He glared at her and shifted the laptop from one arm to another. "No, you look. If you think I'm staying in a nudist colony for a week, you'd better think again." He turned away.

Tasha laughed. "This isn't a nudist colony, it's a Club Regale resort. Eden II. Remember?"

"Those people didn't have clothes on! I'm not so sure about the guy behind the desk, but those people out there in the pool—"

"Oh, he had shorts or something on, I'm sure."

"Well, I'm not sure," he replied. "I'm leaving."

"And miss your vacation?"

"I'll schedule another one."

"But you're here now. Why not stay?"

Andrew stared at her, then shook his head. "If you think after all you've put me through the past six or seven hours I'm going to share my vacation with *you* in a . . . a place where people take their clothes off, then you're just as crazy as I thought you were." He began walking toward the door.

"Whatsamatter? You chicken?"

She thought she could see the tiny hairs on the back of his neck stand straight up. Again he ignored her. Tasha followed.

"C'mon. It's just a week. Stay and loosen up a bit. Do you some good to get out of those stuffy old clothes for a while—kick off those wing tips and bury your toes in the sand, relax, sunbathe. Get in on a little nightlife. Share a Jacuzzi with me. Heck, wear a toga and party all night. Might be fun." She grinned wickedly at him.

"You're crazy," he told her.

"Yeah, I know. You've told me once or twice.

"Look, there's not another bus until morning. It's late. You've been traveling all day and you've got to be tired. Not to mention what jet lag will do to you. At least spend the night and think about it. Just get in your room and stay there for the night. In the morning, things may look different."

"Yeah, I'm tired all right. I'm tired of your being everywhere I am," he said. "I'm tired of your crazy personality, I'm tired of trying to get myself out of messes because of you, and I'm tired of your following me."

"I'm not following you."

Andrew snorted. He faced the hotel and ran the fingers of both hands through his short blond hair, an exasperated look on his face. She wished his hair were just a little longer. She'd like to run her fingers through those golden tresses herself.

She was alarmed with herself for thinking that, but maybe she'd found her ace in the hole. He was tired—maybe of her, but he was tired. It had been a long day, and she wasn't ready to let him go yet. He was a challenge if she ever saw one, and she was up to a challenge any day.

Besides, she had kind of liked the look on his face when his gaze trailed over her body earlier.

"So stay."

He looked at her then for a long, lingering moment. His gaze trailed over her lips and down her neck to the rounded collar of her T-shirt. His chest heaved as he slowly inhaled, and then let his breath out on the breeze. Shivers trailed down her spine. She liked his looking at her like that.

"No!" Shaking his head, he started away from her. "No, I'm not staying. I'm getting the hell out of here and away from you as fast as I can." He stalked off.

"Where do you think you're going?"

"To find another bus out of here."

"Might be a while," she replied.

"I don't care. I'll wait the whole damned night if I have to."

"Are you that eager to get away from me?"

He whirled and faced her dead on. "Yes, ma'am, I am."

Tasha's cheeks grew hot. His bluntness actually hurt. "Well, if that's the way you feel about it, I wouldn't want you to stay. I wouldn't want you to loosen that noose around your neck and live a little. I wouldn't want you to unwrap those mummy clothes and let your skin breathe. You know what? I think you're afraid, Andrew Jacob Powell III, that's what. I think you're afraid of losing a little control. Of having a little fun."

Andrew's gaze narrowed at her. "You don't know a damned thing about me, lady. You damned liberal . . . hippie!"

Anger gathered inside Tasha. "Hippie!" she screeched. "I am absolutely not a hippie! A liberal, yes, but a hippie? No, sir, not me. I'm not a hippie. No."

I like to refer to myself more as a free spirit, thank you. Hippie is passé.

"I bet you're a Democrat to boot, aren't you?" he taunted.

Tasha's hands went to her hips, balled in tight fists. "And damned proud of it, you conservative little—"

He held up his hand. "Don't. Don't say another word."

Tasha chuckled. "You little . . ."

He glared at her.

"You little . . . *Republican!*"

"*What?*"

"You heard me," she confirmed. "I called you a Republican."

"And that's supposed to be an insult?"

"You figure it out."

Andrew's face turned beet red. "Let me tell you about the Republicans, little girl. . . ."

Tasha bit her lip, trying to conceal the smile that was beginning to broaden across her face. While Andrew ranted, her gaze was drawn to a commotion a few yards behind him. Her eyes grew wide with the bubble of laughter trying to explode in her throat. She crossed her arms over her chest to hold it all in while he raved in front of her about the merits of being Republican.

Finally, she could conceal her laughter no longer. It burst out of her in an eruption of giggles that made her bend over at the waist.

Andrew stopped his tirade and stared at her. "What's so damned funny?"

Tasha bit her inner lip to stop her laughter. "You."

He shifted his weight. "Me?"

"Yeah, you."

She could tell Andrew didn't think any of it was funny. "Look, have you no respect? Throughout history the Republicans—"

Tasha shook her head and held up a hand. "I'm not laughing about the Republicans, you dope. I couldn't care less. I'm laughing at what

CRAZY FOR YOU

is going on behind you and how it's going to mess up your plans."

She giggled again and Andrew stared at her. "What in the world are you talking about?"

Still smiling, she replied, "Sorry, but I doubt you'll be going anywhere tonight—or tomorrow, for that matter."

He narrowed his eyes. "What makes you sure about that, Ms. Smarty Pants?"

"Turn around."

When he did, Andrew came face to face with the thing that made her so tickled and was about to make him blow his top.

The picket signs said:

BUS DRIVERS' STRIKE

All the bus drivers were lolling in the parking lot in chaise longues, drinking piña coladas, and listening to reggae.

They were having a wonderful time.

Tasha shrugged. "Guess that settles that."

"Settles what?" The look on Andrew's face was priceless.

"You're staying."

He shook his head in disbelief. "Uh-uh. No."

"Uh-huh," she confirmed.

"I can't stay here. With you. In this place."

Tasha laughed. "You don't have to stay with me, silly. You've got a room, right? What's the big deal? It's late, you're not going to take a bus out of here tonight, and you certainly can't walk out of here. So . . . let's go check in."

He leaned against the side of the hotel. Closing his eyes, Andrew exhaled, long, and shook his head. "I can't believe this is happening," he muttered.

Hooking her arm in his, Tasha slowly led him back toward the lobby doors. He went without a fight.

"I need sleep." He pinched the bridge of his nose. Tasha took in the weariness in his eyes.

"Don't think about it," she offered. "Just think about a hot shower, a comfortable bed, a nice little room just for you. Peaceful bliss. It will be great. In the morning, you can decide what you want to do. I'll even help if you want."

He groaned and nodded. It almost seemed as if he'd allowed himself to slip into a stupor. "In the morning?"

"Yes." They proceeded across the pavement.

He shook his head from side to side as they walked. "I can't take any more of this today," he mumbled as they entered the double doors again.

Tasha patted his arm and smiled. "There, there. It's okay. Just don't think about it right now. I'll take care of everything. Everything will be just fine. I've got something in my bag that works wonders for stressful days like this." She chattered on and Andrew's shoulders slumped in defeat. "It's an herbal combination, very safe, a mixture of nettle leaf, pennyroyal, and uva ursi. . . ."

FOUR

Andrew sheepishly stepped up to the reservation desk. He tried to concentrate only on the tasks at hand. One, get his room; two, get some sleep; three, get out of this godforsaken place first thing in the morning.

He didn't look anywhere other than the face of the man behind the desk. He was a buff-looking specimen, to be sure—muscles bulging, pecs shining, hair slicked back into a shiny blond ponytail—and he was nude, Andrew was sure of it, although he didn't venture a look. To say he made Andrew uncomfortable was an understatement.

One glance at Tasha's reaction to the guy told him all he needed to know. She was practically drooling.

No one, by any stretch of the imagination, could call Andrew Jacob Powell III a prude. Even though his values were conservative, he'd had his share of good times—stretched one or two out to the limits, even—but spending time with nudists was where he drew the line.

He glanced to his right. Tasha smiled back. Of course, she seemed perfectly at ease with the entire scenario. Lord, this probably wasn't an accident for her. She'd probably planned to spend her vacation running around in her birthday suit.

It was not a scenario he wanted to dwell on.

He jerked his gaze back to the clerk. Where did one put a name tag when one was nude? Andrew glanced lower. The nameplate on the desk read *Todd*.

"Sir," Todd interrupted, "we seem to have a bit of a problem."

Why that didn't surprise Andrew, he didn't know. "Let's hear it, Todd."

Todd started to round the counter.

Andrew pushed out his hand. "Stop!"

The man arched a brow at him. "Excuse me?"

"Stop. Don't come out from behind that counter."

Todd edged closer.

"I repeat, don't do it!"

He rounded the corner. Andrew covered his eyes, then quickly turned to Tasha and covered hers.

"Andrew, what the hell are you doing?"

Slowly, Andrew lowered his hands from his eyes and Tasha's, and turned back around. Todd stood next to the counter, wearing long, wildly patterned shorts and sandals.

"Oh." Andrew let out a huge sigh.

Todd arched a brow again. "You were expecting?"

Shaking his head, Andrew turned back to the desk. "Nothing."

Tasha giggled.

He ignored her.

The Adonis look-alike picked up some pamphlets and brochures and went back behind the counter.

Andrew thrust his thumb toward the windowed wall. "Are those people nude out there?"

Todd laughed out loud. "In the pool? Oh, no. Not there. Just looks that way through that glass. The nude pool is further away from the hotel." He looked back down at his paperwork.

Andrew cringed. *Nude pool?*

"And the nude beach and Jacuzzi are adjacent to the regular beach."

Nude beach! Nude Jacuzzi!

"So let's settle this thing with your reservation."

Andrew had a hard time getting his mind off the nude beach. "Yes. My reservation. I need my room immediately." He also needed a handful of aspirin and a nice cool bed.

"We have a slight problem."

Oh, hell. Panic landed heavy on his stomach. "What is it now?"

"We don't seem to have one."

Andrew gritted his teeth. "Don't seem to have what?"

"We have no record of your reservation."

"Impossible." Andrew reached for his briefcase, then mentally swore. "I have a reservation number, but it's"—he tossed Tasha a look—"somewhere in the Atlantic, I assume."

Todd eyed him suspiciously. "It would be under your name, would it not?"

"Yes."

"But it's not."

Andrew closed his eyes. Damn Doug Johnston. "Try Hayward and Pendleton Pharmaceuticals."

He raked his gaze over the books. "Sorry, sir, no."

Andrew gave him several other names. No luck. Heaving a sigh, he replied, "All right. I'll make one now."

Todd tilted his chin upward. "That's impossible."

"Why?"

"All our rooms are full, sir. It's peak season."

Jeez. Of course. "You don't have anything?" Andrew willed himself not to panic. No car, no luggage, no room?

"No, sir. I'm sorry."

Andrew pounded the desk with his fist. "Call me a cab. I'm getting out of here." He paced in front of the desk.

"There is no cab service, sir."

"Then how do I get out of here?"

"Sir, we are deep in Jamaica and there is a bus drivers' strike—"

"You're telling me there's no way out of here?"

"Unless you'd like to hike, swim, or snorkel your way home." Todd chuckled at his own humor.

Andrew wasn't amused.

Staring off past Todd's head, Andrew had forgotten Tasha was at his side until she laid a hand on his forearm.

"Do you have a reservation for Tasha Smith?" she inquired.

Todd smiled at her, then lowered his gaze to

the books, running his finger over the reservation list. "Ah, yes. Here it is, room 214, ocean view, king-sized bed, no smoking. Just one minute and I'll get your key." He turned to the board behind him, and Tasha smiled at Andrew.

"Problem solved," she said.

Andrew eyed her. "What problem is solved?"

"Your reservation problem."

"You're going to give me your room?"

Tasha smiled more broadly and chuckled. "No, but I'll share."

Andrew stepped back and put out his hands. "No. Definitely not. I'll think of something else."

Todd returned and handed the keys to her, along with a welcome packet. "Hope you enjoy your stay, Ms. Smith. Please let us know if you need anything when you get to your room. Dial seven on your phone for my desk." He grinned at her and, smiling broadly back, Tasha took the things from him.

"There is one thing," she asked. "Do you have roll-away beds here?"

"Why, yes, I think we have a couple."

"I'd like one in my room. Mr. Powell will be staying with me until his reservation is straightened out.

Andrew grasped her by the arm. "Now, look, I didn't agree to this."

"But there's nothing else."

"Surely there's something." He turned back to the man. "Surely there's someone else I could room with, even temporarily?"

Todd brought a finger up to his lips. "Yes, I'd forgotten. Perhaps there is someone."

"Is this a male?"

"Oh, yes."

"Does he . . . wear clothes?"

"Um, yes, he does."

"Then I'll take it."

"I'll have to talk to Samuel first, though. He's the resort meditator. A kind, gentle man. I'm sure you'll like him."

Andrew breathed a sigh of relief. Finally, someone halfway normal.

"He doesn't go nude, does he?"

"Oh, no," the clerk replied. "He usually wears a toga."

Tasha laughed. Andrew glared at her.

"Bring me the roll-away," Tasha said.

"Do not bring the roll-away," Andrew countered. "We won't need it."

Tasha lifted one brow. "Oh? Are you planning to share my bed?"

Horrified, Andrew balked. "No! I mean"—his face turned scarlet—"I mean . . ."

The man looked from Andrew to Tasha, who nodded. "I'll have Josh bring one up after a while, just in case. In the meantime, I'll have to talk to Samuel about sharing his room. Perhaps you should go with Ms. Smith in the interim."

"Josh?"

"Yes. Josh. My right-hand man. Jack-of-all-trades around here. Assistant cook, too."

"Can he drive a bus?"

"No, sorry to say. Union contract."

CRAZY FOR YOU 63

"Great," Andrew muttered. "That's just great. I've landed somewhere between Oz and the Bermuda Triangle. Togas. Maintenance men-slash-cooks. Nude beaches. Bus strikes. No room. No luggage." Somewhere along the line, his idea of a plush beach resort was fading. This place appeared to be some sort of wacky cross between *Cheers* and *The Beverly Hillbillies,* Jamaican-style.

Tasha laughed. "At least you still have your laptop."

Andrew glared at her.

Tasha slid the key into the lock and pushed open the door. The hotel was surrounded with trees and dusk was quickly falling, so the room was dark. After crossing the threshold, she pulled back the curtains and slid open the windows on two walls. Immediately the room appeared lighter.

The ocean was visible to her right; the resort recreation area and pool were to her left. The king-size bed occupied nearly one wall, and a huge floor-to-ceiling mirror graced the opposite side. Mirrors were also attached to the ceiling above the bed.

Interesting.

She glanced around. The room's furnishings consisted of two rattan chairs, a small sofa, and an apartment-size refrigerator. The decor was beachy, of course, with a shell motif and potted plants scattered about. Light and breezy. The bedspread was an aqua and mauve shell pattern; the sofa and cushions on the rattan furniture were upholstered in a companion fabric. Curtains of the same gauzy aqua fluttered from the window, and the ocean breeze freshened the room.

Tasha tossed her backpack on the bed and stepped around it to look out the window. "This is nice," she said, more to herself than to Andrew.

His footsteps sounded behind her. "If you like early rain forest," he muttered.

Tasha turned. "You can always go sleep with Samuel."

"I plan to."

Andrew perused the room's interior as Tasha watched his face. She still hadn't figured him out. *Who are you, Andrew Jacob Powell III?*

"I guess it will do . . . temporarily." He brought his gaze back to her face. "Where's the bathroom?"

Tasha turned and took in two doors on the back wall. Upon inspection, they found one led to a walk-in closet, the other to a full bath. Andrew walked inside, fiddled with the toilet handle, and turned on the water in both the sink and shower.

"Well, at least we've got running water—and hot, at that."

"Expecting a little shack out back with a half moon on the door?"

Andrew rolled his eyes and walked away. "At this point, I'm not quite sure what to expect."

Tasha went to the bed and rummaged through her things. She pulled out several items of clothing—shorts, T-shirts, and such—and stashed them in a drawer of the dresser behind her. She glanced at Andrew, who was pacing the other side of the room. A wicked thought came over her.

She picked up a handful of her underwear and started back toward the dresser. "Don't know why I'm even bothering to unpack these things." She glanced quickly at Andrew. "I probably won't be wearing them anyway."

Andrew paced to the left. Tasha turned back to her bag.

"I should unpack the necessities, but I guess I'll stuff most everything back into the backpack and put it in the closet. No use dirtying things that will have to be washed later." She mumbled the words half to herself, half to Andrew, then peeked at him.

He'd stopped in midstride and stared at her.

"What do you mean?"

Tasha straightened, then returned to the dresser. She pulled all her clothing out and began stuffing the garments back into the backpack. "Well, I probably won't be wearing them much, you know. I'll probably spend most of my time, er, sunbathing. I plan to check out that nude beach. Of course, being the exhibitionist I am. . . ."

Andrew cleared his throat and stepped closer. Reaching forward, he grasped some of her clothes and put them back in the dresser drawer. "You most certainly will need clothing."

"What for?" Tasha goaded. She wanted to smile so badly her mouth hurt. "Oh, by the way, what do *you* plan to do for clothing? Of course, you most likely won't need much. I mean, a swimsuit, maybe, and something to wear at night. Unless you plan to frequent the toga parties, in which case I'm sure we can find an extra sheet around here. Maybe a pair of shorts to wear during the day. Need help shopping?"

Andrew threw his hands in the air and walked away. "I'll handle my clothing situation, thank you! The fact I have no clothing is not *my* choice. You have clothes. Wear them."

"Why? No one except you knows me here, and we don't *really* know each other, do we? What does it matter? Think about it. Why don't we let our hair down and try it?"

"You're stark raving mad, aren't you?" His face was wild.

"I don't think so."

Tasha looked Andrew up, then down. *Boy, does the man need a vacation. He's wound tighter than a drum. Has to be stress. He'll be a challenge,* she reminded herself, *but maybe, just maybe, this vacation hasn't been a waste.* Maybe she could help this man ease back into life a bit and escape the business world for a few days.

"What are you thinking?" he prodded.

"I'm wondering—"

"Stop wondering! Stop looking at me like you want to know what I'd look like without my clothes!"

Tasha chuckled. "That's a switch."

"What do you mean? I don't look at you like that!"

Turning back to the dresser, she picked up her clothing again. One corner of her mouth lifted. "I didn't necessarily mean you. Women in general usually feel men are undressing them with their eyes. Does it make you uncomfortable?"

"Yes. It makes me damned uncomfortable. Stop it."

Tasha laughed again. "For your information, I wasn't doing that. I was just thinking you need this vacation more than most people." She stepped closer. "I don't know how you ended up here, but you did. Obviously, it was a mistake. I, on the other hand, knew pretty much what I was getting into. This trip was a gift from my mother—imagine that! I plan on having the time of my life the next few days. Since you, at the moment, have no choice in the matter, you might consider doing the same."

"But—"

"I don't know you, and you don't know me. When we leave this place, we'll never see each other again. More than likely, we'll never see anyone connected to this place again. So I plan to spend the next five days relaxing and doing whatever I like. If I decide to try nudity as a change of pace, I'm not hurting anyone, and no one is hurting me."

"I'm not—"

"So you can sit here, Andrew Jacob Powell III, grumble over your misfortune, and pine away the remainder of the week, or you can take that noose off your neck and hang loose for a few days. Makes no difference to me. But let me tell you this: I didn't come all the way here to hole myself up in this hotel room. If you're as smart as you appear to be, you won't, either."

When she stopped talking, she was facing Andrew, barely inches separating their faces. "So what do you have to say about that?"

Andrew just stood there. Speechless.

By the time Josh had delivered the roll-away bed and told Andrew that Samuel was not to be found, Tasha was starved. Josh, who turned out to be a Jamaican Jed Clampett look-alike, complete with bib overalls and a floppy straw hat, stood in the doorway of their cabin. Tasha was glad he was fully dressed, but she wouldn't have told Andrew that.

If the truth be known, she wasn't any more keen on this nudity thing than he was. She was no more anxious to take off her clothes in front of perfect strangers than the average female would be. But she couldn't help teasing Andrew. He was so cute when he looked bewildered, and she could tell he thought she was the oddest human being ever to come along the pike.

Well, she guessed she wasn't quite like everyone else, but he would just have to take her or leave her.

"Josh, how do we get something to eat in this place?" Tasha inquired.

The older man brought a hand up to his stubbled chin, pulled at it, and looked at the floor. After a slow minute, he raised his gaze. "Well, seeing as how you've probably not had time to get settled in yet, you haven't read your information packet, have you?"

Tasha glanced to the bed. The packet was still lying there, unopened. "No, I haven't."

"Well . . ." He scratched his head and drawled, "there's the cafeteria downstairs, but it's been closed since eight o'clock. Of course, you could probably find some appetizers at one of the bars."

Tasha glanced at her watch. Nine-thirty-five. She eyed Josh. She really wasn't up to nightlife at the moment. She doubted Andrew was, either. "Now, Josh, didn't I hear something about your being the assistant cook?"

An easy grin spread over his face. "Now that you might have heard. Care to come see what we can dig up?"

Tasha nodded and glanced at Andrew. "Want to come?"

He sat in the rattan chair on the far side of the room. She guessed Josh's news about Samuel didn't help matters any. Ever since they'd arrived and Tasha had goaded him about going nude, he'd sat and muttered about all the injustices he'd been dealt the past twenty-four hours. Tasha just let him grumble. In the meantime, she'd taken a shower and organized her belongings. Now she was ready for something to eat.

"Bring me back something," he muttered.

"Afraid you're gonna see something you don't want to see?"

He shrugged and turned away from her in the seat. Tasha chuckled and followed Josh out the door.

* * *

Andrew hadn't realized how hungry he was. With all the turmoil, he hadn't stopped to think about eating. When Tasha brought in the two large turkey salad sandwiches on sliced sourdough bread, a small bag of potato chips, and two bottles of iced tea, he could have kissed her.

He could have kissed Josh, as well.

He'd taken the twenty minutes or so they were away to assess his situation. He always came up with the same conclusion. There was nothing he could do about any of it, not at the moment, anyway. It was possible he'd have to stay the night with Tasha. Tomorrow, though, he was getting out of here, one way or another.

But right now, the turkey salad sandwich Tasha had set on the dresser looked mighty tempting.

Josh slipped out the door with a promise to return when he had news about Samuel's room, and Andrew turned to Tasha.

"Thanks for the food."

She nodded, sitting cross-legged in the middle of the bed, which she had already claimed as her own, chewing on her sandwich.

"The chips are yours," she called out.

He picked up the sandwich and the chips. "I'll share."

She shook her head. "No, I don't eat them."

Sitting down on the folded out roll-away, he began unwrapping his sandwich. He glanced up at her. "Why?"

"I only eat fresh or steamed vegetables if I can help it."

"Oh." He took a bite. His stomach growled. Finally, food.

"Are you a vegetarian?"

Tasha smiled. "Last time I checked, turkey wasn't a vegetable."

After swallowing, Andrew replied, "Dumb question."

"I do eat very little meat," she added. "Absolutely no red meat. A little poultry and fish now and then. But I eat mostly grains and fruits and vegetables."

"Are you some kind of health nut?" She was *some* kind of nut.

She shook her head again, after taking another bite. "No. I own an organic food store. I sell fresh organically grown fruits and vegetables, some herbs, vitamins, natural remedies, essential oils. That sort of thing. The name of the store is *Naturally.*"

She grinned and Andrew returned the smile. "Of course."

Tasha finished her sandwich and took a drink of tea. "What do you do for a living, Andrew?"

She'd turned the tables entirely and it took him a minute to refocus. "Oh, I'm in pharmaceuticals."

Laughter exploded from Tasha's throat.

"Why is that so funny?"

She covered her mouth with her hand. "It's not, really. I guess I should have known."

"Should have known what?" Damn, he hated it when she laughed at him.

"Oh, the laptop, the clothing, your demeanor.

I should have known. All business. Haven't you ever heard that all work and no play makes Andrew a dull boy?"

The back of Andrew's neck was getting hot. "So I'm dull?"

Tasha cocked her head to one side and stared at him. Slowly, a grin spread across her face. "Maybe," she replied. "But if we work on it, we might be able to change that."

She tossed the unopened stack of literature on Andrew's bed. He glanced up.

"What's all that?" He continued eating.

"Information," she answered.

"About what?"

"About the resort. Aren't you in the least interested?"

"Oh yeah," he yawned. "Let me have it. I can't wait to read about the advantages of walking around naked as a blue jay on the beach and in the rain forest."

She leaned back on one elbow while leafing through one of the pamphlets. The creak of the bedsprings brought his thoughts back to the present.

"Says here nudity is the ultimate oneness with nature. What do you think about that?"

Andrew shrugged his shoulders and glanced away. He didn't give a damn at the moment about listening to what she was planning. "Where did you get all that stuff?"

Tasha turned her face up to him and smiled radiantly. "In the information packet. Want to hear more?"

"Not really," he grumbled, then sat up. He stretched his arms up and around, then stood. Stepping closer to the window, he pulled back the draperies, then snapped them shut again. There were people way out there on a distant beach. Were they nude? He started to perspire.

How disgusting.

"This one says nudity is an incredibly invigorating experience, that it's a growth of the body and soul, that the loss of one's inhibitions helps you find an internal peace." Tasha dropped the pamphlet to her lap and looked at him. "How beautiful! Don't you think so?"

Andrew glanced back at her. "Beautiful?"

"Sure. Don't you see? Being nude makes one forget about all the external trappings of our society. We don't need fancy clothing or jewels or even incredible model's bodies to be at one with ourselves. All we need is what we were born with—and, of course, an acceptance that you are what you are and there ain't a dang thing you can do about it. They're even offering a first-timers' orientation tomorrow morning. We'll have to sign up. What do you think?"

Andrew grimaced. "I think that's hogwash! They're saying that stuff so people will come out here and pay good money to run around naked, ogling each other under the guise of *oneness with nature*. Don't you realize those people out there are a bunch of perverts!"

Tasha rose, dropped the literature to the floor, and stepped closer to him. "Andrew! I know no such thing! Those people out there aren't perverts, they're just nice, ordinary people who don't give a damn what they look like on the outside. They look to the inner self, the inner spirit. Clothing is simply an outer trapping they've decided to cast off."

"You're kidding yourself, Tasha. Those people are only out for one thing—one wild, decadent, and crazy free-for-all of a week. They don't care what they do or who they do it to. And you're a little tofu-fruity in the head if you think for one minute I will cast off my *outer trappings* to release my inner spirit. That's bunk!"

Tasha glared back. "You need to loosen up a little, you know that? Shake a little of that conservatism out your system."

"I may be conservative, but I can loosen up," he challenged. "I can be the life of the damned party if I want to."

Tasha chuckled and crossed her arms over her chest. She toed the carpet in front of her with her bare foot, then pulled her gaze straight up to his face. "We're about as far apart as two people can get, aren't we?"

He turned and stomped away. "Looks like it."

"I guess it's hopeless."

"Probably."

"You watch Rush Limbaugh?"

"Occasionally." He glanced back at her with a puzzled expression. "What's that got to do with anything?"

"You agree with him?"

"For the most part."

CRAZY FOR YOU 75

"Would you ever vote for a woman president?" she taunted.

"There's not a woman in politics today who is a likely candidate."

"Says who?"

"Says me."

And who are you to say?" Tasha edged closer to him, her arms tight across her chest.

"I'm the voice of most of conservative America."

"Yeah, well, most of conservative America can go to hell in a handbasket for all I care."

Andrew felt his ire rising. "You think you're so damned smart, don't you? You want to get into issues, lady, I can sure as hell get into some issues with you. And I'll tell you what, I'll bet we're on the opposite side of the fence on every single one of them."

"Shoot." Her eyes narrowed.

"Abortion."

"Pro-choice," Tasha stated adamantly.

"Pro-life," he countered.

"Health care reform," Tasha hurled at him.

"A waste of money."

"Environmental issues?"

"Eats at my craw."

Tasha huffed off to the other side of the room, her back to him. She didn't want to talk about it anymore. She didn't want to talk to him anymore. This wasn't going to work.

Not at all.

"We're total opposites," Andrew said. "Sharing this room will never work. I sure as hell hope Josh gets here with the key to Samuel's room soon. Very soon."

Tasha let her eyes meet his and nodded ever so slightly. "Can't be soon enough for me."

For a moment, they stared at one another. Finally, Andrew broke the silence. "If I could, I'd leave this minute. If it weren't for the bus strike, I'd be out of here by now."

Tasha nodded. "Yeah, well, and I'd probably help you." She started for the door.

"Where are you going?"

"Taking a walk."

"On the beach?"

"No, in the air." She stepped over the threshold.

"Be . . . careful. Watch out for—"

The door slammed behind her.

"Crazy nudists," he mumbled.

A few seconds later a knock sounded at the door. Andrew angrily crossed the room to answer it. "Forget your key or something? Serves you right, you know, for leaving in such a snit."

Josh stood on the threshold.

After a moment, he said, "Samuel has returned and has agreed to share his room—temporarily. You see, on Thurs—"

"At last." Andrew sighed deeply and gathered up his laptop, brushing by Josh on his way out.

Was this it? Would he see her again?

More than likely, he would not. Thank God.

Glancing back into the room, a pang of something he didn't want to describe raced across his belly.

Hard to say, though, he thought. With Tasha, one should probably always be prepared for anything.

FIVE

Night sounds skittered outside the window as Andrew lay in his bed and thought about how he'd survived the day. Things had changed, though, and he wasn't quite sure if they'd changed in the direction he'd wanted.

He'd been attracted to Tasha from the beginning, that was a fact. What man wouldn't be? It had been a physical, lustful need to get close to her body, to feel her in his hands—even if she was a lunatic.

Funny, he thought as he smiled at the ceiling, she suddenly didn't seem crazy as much as sexy and outrageous and downright appealing.

Oh, hell. . . .

I should get out of here, he thought, *before anything happens I'll regret.* But he couldn't. At last report, Josh said, the bus strike would probably last the week, or longer. No one seemed to know.

He was stuck.

Andrew rolled onto his side, the night breeze warm and sultry through his window. He stared across the room at Samuel, sleeping in the other twin bed, his form silhouetted against a moonbeam slicing in the opposite window. The older man's rhythmic breathing lifted his chest slowly, evenly.

He was an odd man who spoke little and gave the impression of indifference to his new roommate. Samuel had made it clear, however, that he didn't expect this arrangement to last longer than a day or two. He assured Andrew that something would open up, soon.

Andrew wasn't sure of that. In fact, he wasn't sure of anything anymore, particularly when it came to Tasha Smith.

Maybe he was reading more into this than was there. There was nothing between them but a physical thing that probably wouldn't go past the end of the week.

Besides, they were much too opposite for anything permanent to develop between them. But for once in his life, maybe he *should* fly by the seat of his pants and just see what happened—for the next few days, at least. It could be fun.

He didn't know if it was in him to do anything more.

"I'm not going in there." Andrew stopped short at the side entrance to the hotel.

"But, Andrew," Tasha pleaded, "I have no inhibitions about all this. You're the one who needs the orientation. Come on, give it a chance, won't you?"

Tasha wasn't quite sure how she'd managed to get Andrew out of Samuel's hotel room, but she had. It was going to take more coaxing on her part before he made his way down the hallway to the meeting room. She hooked her arm in his and stepped forward.

"Remember," she added convincingly, "the brochure said all participants will benefit from this brief orientation to the resort. It's for those who are hesitant and unsure about, um . . . about all the activities offered, remember? For the faint of heart. I think you fall into that category." She patted his arm as they approached the thick wooden door. "Don't worry, I'll be right beside you."

Andrew glared at her. "That's not very comforting."

"Why?" She feigned surprise.

"Because you're crazy and I don't know what the hell I'm doing here."

Tasha grinned and opened the outside door of the lodge. "We agreed, Andrew, that while we're here, we might as well try this thing. Remember? We talked about it this morning." She'd wakened him just after the crack of dawn. Samuel had already left for the day.

"I was half asleep. Needed my coffee."

"That's no excuse. We'll just see how the orientation goes, all right? Just trust me."

"Trust *you*?" Andrew echoed as he cautiously stepped inside. "That's like asking me to trust a rattlesnake."

Tasha smiled and led him down the hall.

The room was somewhat secluded and located near the back of the building. Good, Andrew thought. He wasn't into meeting up with unclothed humans at the moment.

Upon entering the empty, red-carpeted room, Tasha led him up the aisle between several rows of chairs, then plopped herself down smack in the center of the front row. Andrew shrank back.

"I believe I'll sit in the back." He turned toward the rear of the room.

"Andrew Powell! Get back up here and sit with me. Aren't you at all interested in this?"

Andrew turned and scowled at her. "You don't want me to answer that truthfully, do you?"

"Yes, I do."

"No, I don't think you do." He turned toward the last row.

"An-drew." Tasha drew out the two syllables of his name.

Andrew sat in the far right corner. He grinned triumphantly at her. "Ye-es?" he mimicked.

She stared at him for a moment before turning back to her seat with a harrumph. "I don't know why I even bother."

Andrew listened to her mutter from across the room.

"You'd think he'd want to expand his horizons a bit and experience something beyond the norm while he had the chance." Her voice rose. "Especially when he's in a situation where no one knows him. But no-o-o-o, not that conservative little—"

"I think that's quite enough, Tasha," Andrew warned. As irritated as he was that she had dragged him down here this morning, he didn't want to get into another sparring match with her.

Tasha sat silently for a minute. She squirmed in her seat. He could tell he was making her extremely agitated. Fine. It was time the tables were turned.

"But you could give this thing a whirl. There's nothing to be ashamed of, is there?" She still faced the front. Andrew watched her back. Suddenly, she whirled in her seat and pinned him with her stare. "Is there? You don't have anything you're ashamed of, Andrew, do you?" she questioned, her tone almost sarcastic.

Andrew smiled sweetly at her. "Ashamed? Actually, I'm fearful of the shock value, my dear Tasha. I try to be modest most of the time, you see, but the size of—"

The door to the room burst open. "My, my, my, my, my! We have guests!" A middle-aged man with a Caesar haircut and a toga draped over his body swiftly entered the room and, while clapping his hands, made his way to the front. Andrew caught and held Tasha's heated gaze. He watched her flush, then abruptly turn in her seat to face front.

Samuel had arrived.

"Greetings! Greetings to one and all! Oh, my," Andrew's roommate proclaimed, "it is such a beautiful morning out there, is it not?" He leaned closer to Tasha as if sharing something in secrecy. "I'm itching to get out there myself, you know. The weather is simply perfect!" He abruptly straightened, then thrust his hand out toward

Tasha. Andrew couldn't see her face, but he was sure she was smiling as she took his hand. "Good morning, my pretty. My name is Samuel."

"Good morning to you. I'm Tasha." Andrew thought Tasha's voice was way too cheerful. What the hell was she doing? The man was obviously an idiot. Who else would be seen in a toga, for God's sake?

"Give me a break," Andrew breathed. He wasn't going to hang around too long for this little exchange.

Samuel took a step back and glanced at Andrew. "You may move to the front, sir, if you so choose. I assure you, I won't bite!"

Tasha giggled, but didn't look his way. Andrew sat up straighter in his seat. "I'm fine where I am. Thank you, Samuel."

Samuel glanced from Tasha to Andrew. "Well, if it suits you, then it suits me. To each his own!" He fluttered his right hand out in the air. "That's pretty much the name of the game around here, you know. Anything goes!"

Turning, Samuel approached a rise and stepped up one step. "Let's begin, shall we? I assume this is the first time for both of you, so we'll get right to it. I just love virgins, you know. I mean, virgins to the resort. Oh, dear, I think I made a faux pas. You don't know how lucky you are you didn't get Samantha. She's my twin sister and all, but sometimes she smacks a bit of the wild side." He grinned at Tasha and glanced at Andrew.

Andrew snorted. A bit of the wild side? What the hell did he think he smacked of?

"Of course, she's out of the country for a few days. Relatives, you know. They can be quite demanding."

So can strangers, Andrew thought.

"It's simple, really," Samuel continued. "There is only one thing I can tell you about experiencing our activities, and that is to simply let your mind go. The key is relaxation. You must relax in order to expand your mind. Here at Eden II, you should allow yourself to experience your heart's desire. Allow yourself to do the things you normally would not do. Remember, it all stays here, my pretties, at the week's end." He smiled, closed his eyes, and stretched his arms out in front of him.

Tasha followed suit.

"Yes," Samuel whispered, "let the mind go. Try it with me now, everyone. Repeat after me. Ummm. Ummmm."

Tasha closed her eyes and hummed right along with Samuel. Andrew studied her pert, upturned profile, her lashes lying soft against her skin, the sleek arch of her neck somehow inviting. What would she do if he got the chance to trail his lips down her neck from just under her chin to her collarbone? How would her skin taste? How would her hair smell?

Samuel cleared his throat and Andrew tore his gaze from Tasha's neck to Samuel's face. His right eye was arched open and he was staring at Andrew while he continued humming. Andrew had the damnedest feeling Samuel could read his thoughts.

"Everybody now. With me," he repeated as he held his hands out palm up in front of him, his thumb and forefinger meeting. His open eye was still trained on Andrew. "Ummmm. Ummmmm. Relax now."

Andrew didn't move a muscle. For about the thirtieth time that week, he had to ask how he'd allowed himself to get into this cuckoo's nest. Why didn't he just find a way out of here and leave?

His gaze again drifted to Tasha. Damn. If he'd admit it to himself, he already knew the answer to that question. Tasha Smith intrigued him as no other woman had in his adult life, and that was saying something.

"The secret to losing oneself in our activities," Samuel continued, his eyes now closed, his face pointing to the heavens, "is to become one with nature. Realize the joy of shedding one's inhibitions. Realize the trappings society has put on the human being, the inner soul, the embarrassment suffered daily by countless thousands who feel they must clothe their naked bodies and hide from the truth. Realize that with the shedding of one's inhibitions, the true self emerges and one must open up his heart to delve into the inner sanctity of being and not thrive on the decorations one places on the soul."

"Give me a break," Andrew breathed, the words barely audible. He shifted his position in the chair.

"And realize," Samuel droned on, "one must set a personal goal, serve himself with a personal vendetta against the evils society has cast upon us at the misunderstanding of our mission here. Our objective is not one of judging by the beauty of another's body, but by the gift one receives by exposing bodily imperfections to the world, thus making our spirit cleansed and purified and our soul fed with the richness of our naked existence, and our psyche less vulnerable."

"What a crock of—" Andrew stopped in mid mutter as the door to his left opened. Two men stepped boldly into the room, spotted Tasha sitting at the front, and made their way down the aisle toward her, all the while snickering under their breath. They sat in the row directly behind her.

For a moment, Andrew could barely believe his eyes. It couldn't be true. Those SOBs! Doug Johnston and Brett Southworth, his colleagues from Seattle, the ones who had arranged this travesty, were *here!* What the hell did they think they were doing?

Samuel droned on, but for the life of him Andrew couldn't decipher a single word. Tasha was engrossed in Samuel's musings. She was sitting Indian fashion in her chair now. It seemed her long, tanned legs were wrapped around the chair. Andrew swallowed. Those damned irresistible legs.

Her hands rested on her knees, palms upward, thumb and finger meeting, mimicking Samuel. Her face was turned to the ceiling, her eyes still closed. Andrew wasn't sure, but he thought he could hear a faint hum coming from her throat.

Behind her, Doug and Brett were watching every move she made and punching each other in the ribs. Their eyes were raking over her body. Damn those bastards! They were trying to imagine what she would look like in the buff!

Abruptly, the humming stopped. Samuel opened his eyes and lowered his hands. He stared straight ahead to Doug and Brett. After a moment's hesitation, Tasha opened her eyes and lowered her feet to the floor. She seemed in a trance, her gaze fixed on Samuel.

Suddenly, Samuel appeared agitated and Andrew leaned forward in his seat.

"Excuse me, gentlemen," Samuel said, "your aura has interrupted my meditation. I'm going to have to ask you to exit the room." He waved his hand in the direction of the door. Tasha glanced a bit to her right.

Doug and Brett simply sat—and smiled.

"Sirs, I am speaking to you!" Andrew couldn't believe Samuel could actually raise his voice, but he did. "You must speak to the receptionist for a refund. Your intentions here are not honorable. You must leave now."

Doug and Brett looked at each other, then Doug guffawed. He rose. "Now look here . . ." Doug appeared to be searching for a name.

As if Samuel read his mind, he quickly replied, "Samuel. My name is Samuel."

"All right, *Samuel*. Let me see if I've got this straight. Because you don't like our aura, you feel our intentions here may not be honorable and you're asking us to leave?"

Samuel nodded. "Sir, that is what I feel and what I asked. Now, if you please, Miss Tasha and I need to continue. Her aura is quite pleasant, you know, and pure."

Brett stood and jabbed Doug in the ribs. "Pleasant, I'm sure," he snickered. "But I wonder—"

At that instant, Tasha rose to face the two men. Andrew recognized the angry expression and saw her mouth open. He was sure she was just about ready to blast the two of them, but she didn't get the chance. Somehow, he'd made it to his feet, hurdled two rows of chairs, and was standing with a hand on Brett's shoulder. Startled, Brett turned around.

Andrew's fist curled around Brett's shirt collar. "You shouldn't make judgment calls about someone you know nothing about, Southworth."

To say both Brett and Doug were startled was one thing, but after several seconds slid by, Andrew thought he was probably the most startled of all. Never had he approached a coworker in such a manner. But then, this wasn't work.

"Well, well, Andrew Powell. You *are* here."

Andrew loosened his grip on Brett and shifted his gaze to Doug Johnston. Doug watched him, a sneer on his face.

"The question is," Andrew returned without a second thought, "why are you here?"

Doug and Brett shared a glance. "Vacation," they both supplied at once, as if rehearsed.

Andrew stepped away and studied each of them

with narrowed eyes. He crossed his arms over his chest. "Why do I have difficulty believing that?"

Doug shrugged. "Don't know, Andrew, my boy. Once we'd made the arrangements for you to come here, we couldn't resist checking it out for ourselves. It was an opportunity we couldn't pass up." Doug glanced again to Tasha and grinned hungrily. "No, sir. Just didn't think we could pass it up."

Andrew pulled his gaze away from the two men and glanced at Tasha, who stood slightly away from all of them. She had a puzzled look on her face, but when Doug turned to smile at her, she offered a half grin back. In that instant, Andrew felt as though the temperature of his blood rose two hundred degrees.

When Tasha's gaze hesitantly met his, he saw something he didn't want to see. Damn it! Was that some sort of desire in her eyes for Doug Johnston? Suddenly he felt like a fool. Tasha obviously went after any man who gave her a second glance. How could he have been so stupid?

Andrew didn't bother to give an explanation. He simply turned and walked out the room.

"Well, if you aren't about the rudest man I've ever met!"

Tasha burst into Samuel's hotel room. Angry didn't even begin to describe the emotion coursing through her body at the moment.

Andrew stepped away and crossed the room. Abruptly, he turned to face her. "All right, Tasha.

What is it now? Doug drop you like a hot potato and you're back looking for handouts?"

After crossing her arms over her chest, Tasha stood firmly in front of him. Nothing was going to make her budge until she got the answers she was seeking, not even his arrogance.

"What are you talking about, Andrew? I don't know those men. Obviously, though, you do. Just spill the whole nine yards and get it over with. Who are they and why are you acting like an idiot?"

"Idiot?" Andrew angrily stepped closer. "I don't know who you're calling an idiot! I'm the only sane person around here. You don't see me meditating in front of some strange man who hums and feels up everyone else's aura, do you? Didn't you find that just a teensy bit strange, Tasha? Hell, you can't think that's normal."

Tasha met and held Andrew's gaze. She'd never seen him so animated, and she'd seen him pretty darned animated. Andrew Jacob Powell III was agitated. Why, she couldn't figure out, and she wasn't leaving until she did.

"Leave Samuel out of this. He's a nice man and I found him quite pleasant. At least he doesn't shout at me."

Andrew threw up his arms and stalked away from her.

"You never answered my question. Who are those men, and why are you so angry with me?"

He spun back to face her. "Angry? I'll tell you why I'm angry. You were giving Doug Johnston the eye. Don't deny it. I saw every bit of it. He was coming on to you and you were giving the old invite right back. I'll bet you've already made a date with him for later, haven't you? I bet you can't wait to drag him to some toga party or . . . or worse, to some nude beach. And he won't balk, either."

There were a lot of words ready to jump out of Tasha's throat, but she choked back every one of them. Biting her tongue to keep silent, she studied Andrew before replying. This whole conversation was ridiculous. There was a whole lot more here than met the eye.

Tasha took a deep breath and crossed her arms. "Who is Doug Johnston?" she asked calmly, pinning him with her stare. "Just answer that for me, please."

Hands on his hips, Andrew glanced away and sighed. His shoulders relaxed at the gesture and Tasha felt a little of the ice about him melt. "He's a colleague of mine from Seattle. We work in the same firm."

"And what about the other one?"

Andrew looked at her and huffed another breath. "Yeah. Him, too."

"What are they doing here?"

Andrew threw up his hands and rolled his eyes. "How the hell do I know? For all I know, they could be carrying out some big plan to catch me naked with—"

Tasha watched his eyes widen. Suddenly, they narrowed to slits and he moved closer to her. For an instant, Tasha was almost fearful of the look on his face.

"You're in on this, aren't you?" he snarled.

"What?"

"You're in on it. You, Doug, Brett—you're all working together, aren't you?"

"I don't know what you're talking about!" Tasha stepped back.

Andrew followed and grasped both her arms at the elbow. "I understand it now. They probably hired you before I even got on the plane. All that stuff with the rental car, throwing away my luggage, this crazy place—it was all planned, wasn't it?"

"I don't think anyone could think up something so bizarre if they tried."

"And you! Acting like you're taking me under your wing and helping me lose my inhibitions. You're too eager, Tasha, just too eager. What is it? Do you have a camera hidden somewhere? Were you going to get pictures of me nude? Were you going to blackmail me with them?"

Tasha shook her head in confusion. "Andrew," she said, "you're not making a lick of sense. Why would I want to take pictures of you nude? Well, now I've had time to think about it . . . ahem, I mean, really, Andrew, why would I want to blackmail you? I barely know you. I wanted to save you from a life of boredom and spice up my life at the same time. I thought maybe we could be friends, maybe even more than that for a while. But blackmail—that's absolutely ludicrous. If you think for one minute—"

Andrew stomped off and ran every finger of both hands through his short hair. "Would you just shut up for a minute? Doug and Brett *would* try to blackmail me. Don't you see? They want me out of the firm. I'm too much competition for them!"

Tasha let the room fall silent. Andrew paced the length of the bed three times before he stopped and returned his gaze to her face. Tasha eyed him, wondering why any man would get so worked up about something like this. Why would any man put himself in a position with his career where others would try to blackmail him to get a job promotion or snag his job? To her way of thinking, it was ridiculous. Poor Andrew.

"That may be true, but let's get one thing straight," she began softly. "For one, I don't know those two men and don't care to. They didn't hire me to do anything. I have no idea if they're out to blackmail you or not, I just know I have nothing to do with it. And I don't have the *hots* for either one of them. I'm not interested in getting anyone out of his clothes—at the moment."

Her voice rose a bit. She hadn't intended to get angry, but the more she thought about it, the more his accusations angered her. "Least of all Doug Johnston, Brett Whomever, or *you*, Andrew Powell. All I want right now is to go back to my room, slip back between the sheets of my wonderful king-sized bed and take a nap. When I'm finished, then maybe you and I can sit down and talk about the real reason you're so damned angry!"

SIX

"The real reason I'm so angry? What the hell is that supposed to mean?"

Andrew stared at Tasha's back as she left the room.

The real reason I'm so angry? Give me a break!

There were all kinds of reasons he should be angry. For one thing, getting caught up in this mess would make any man angry. For another thing, Doug and Brett were here for a reason—and he didn't know why. He couldn't have been right earlier, could he? Could Doug and Brett really be trying to blackmail him out of his job? He didn't know. He didn't want to think about it, because when he did, he got angrier.

His job was extremely important to him. He needed it for more than financial security. He needed it because he needed the identification with his career, because of the workaholic thing—he was his job and his job was him. Without his work, he was nothing. He needed the competitiveness, the camaraderie. He needed the damned security being a top-notch businessman gave him.

Bottom line: He needed the damned job to

make him feel good about himself, to make him feel complete.

See anything wrong with this picture, Powell?

Startled, Andrew turned and glanced about the room. The voice belonging to those words wasn't his, but Tasha's. He could swear she'd spoken and had to stare at the door to make sure she wasn't still standing there. Damn it, she was invading his mind, too.

He shook his head to rid it of her voice and the direction of his thoughts. Right now, he had other things to think about. He wasn't going to let Tasha's nagging get to him at the moment. He had to think about why Doug and Brett were here.

They were a constant threat to his job security. He'd known that for a long time. They'd never been able to reach the success his team had in sales, and they'd probably do just about anything to oust him from the company—or at least help him down the ladder a bit.

Andrew sat on the bed and expelled an irritated sigh. He pounded the center of one of the pillows. The thought of those two scheming for his job made him even angrier. If Doug and Brett were out to play dirty, he might have to play hardball. He couldn't do anything to risk his job, but he wouldn't hand it to them on a silver platter, either.

But was that the anger to which Tasha referred? Somehow, he didn't think so. Tasha didn't know much about his job or about Doug and Brett. He was sorry he'd accused her of working with them against him. If he'd learned one thing about Tasha Smith the past day, it was that she was completely honest, so much so she blurted out every thought with utter openness. She couldn't be hiding anything like that from him.

He had to apologize.

Then what else could have made him so angry a few minutes earlier? What did Tasha mean?

It hit him like a bolt of lightning. Even if he didn't want to admit it, he knew exactly what she was talking about. He was jealous. Doug had slid Tasha a grin, and she had reciprocated. He'd jumped to conclusions and the green-eyed monster had taken control of his emotions.

Damn. He was jealous. Now he had to apologize for two things instead of one. And he better do it as quickly as possible.

Someone was knocking on her door. Tasha pulled the sheets over her ears.

"Go away. I don't want any," she mumbled.

There was a hesitant silence. The knocking began again. If she just ignored him, maybe he would go away. She wasn't in the mood to spar with Andrew once more.

The knocking grew louder.

"Go away!"

She pulled the pillow over her head. The only thing she accomplished was muffling the persistent knock. Finally, she flung the covers back and jumped from the bed. Hastily, she padded across the room while running a hand through her mussed hair.

"You sure are a tenacious little jerk, Andrew Powell," she muttered as her hand curled around the doorknob. "You'd better have an apology ready to jump from your lips," she said a little louder as she pulled open the door.

But Andrew wasn't standing on the other side of the threshold; the two men from Seattle were.

"Apology?" The one called Doug stepped forward and smiled. "I don't recall having anything to apologize to you about. Did I miss something earlier?"

Tasha dropped her arm to her side. Momentarily, she was taken aback. Where was Andrew? What was she going to do with these two jerks?

"What do you want?" she returned bluntly, leaning against the door jamb with crossed arms. She was in no mood for the two of them.

Doug stepped forward. "We thought we could interest you in a swim or a lively game of volleyball. Or, if you don't have plans for later, we're heading to the disco. Want to join us? We got in early this morning, and I understand you've been here for a day already. Would you like to show us around?"

Tasha didn't miss a beat. "There are employees for that. Sorry, not interested." She reached for the door and started to close it. The other man reached forward and laid a hand on the doorknob. Tasha stared at him. The gall!

"You'll have to excuse me, but I'm busy at the

moment." She started to push the door closed again.

He resisted, smiling all the while.

"Do you mind?" She glared at him.

For several seconds, her gaze met his. Finally, he took his hand from the door and backed up a few steps.

"I'm sorry. Where are our manners?" Doug intervened sarcastically. She could understand why Andrew didn't like the man. "We haven't properly introduced ourselves. My name is Doug Johnston and this is Brett Southworth. We're actually friends of Andrew's. Work in the same firm, you know. And you are . . ."

"Not interested, like I said. Look, if you're friends of Andrew's, go get him to show you around. He's here somewhere. He never ventures too far away." Tasha couldn't help the dig, but immediately felt sorry she'd said it.

She glanced up and saw Andrew heading toward them. *Damnation.* She didn't like the look on his face.

"In fact, there he is now," she said coldly. "Maybe I'll see you around." With that, she slammed the door between them and quickly threw the dead bolt. As she leaned against the door, she realized she was breathing hard. She didn't like those two men.

Well, Andrew would just have to hash it out with them himself. It wasn't her problem.

The knock came again.

Surely those two hadn't the audacity to come back for a repeat performance. If so, she wasn't going to give them the time of day. Tasha rose from the bed. Just a quick peek through the peephole.

This time it was Andrew, and his face didn't look any softer. In fact, he looked about ready to explode.

Tasha quickly opened the door. Andrew's fist was raised in midknock.

"You know, if you don't get that scowl off your face, it could freeze like that."

Andrew glared and strode past her into the room.

Slowly, she closed the door and turned, resting her back against the cool wood. The hour or so they'd been apart obviously had done nothing to quell his anger.

"So, Andrew, is something on your mind?" Tasha pinned him with her stare as he finally stopped pacing and met her gaze.

"Cut the crap, Tasha. Let's get on with this."

"Okay, let's. What's on your mind?"

"What's on my mind is you—and those two. What the hell were they doing here?"

Tasha studied him for a minute as she chewed the inside of her lip. He was stressed to the max. Had the arrival of those two done that to him?

"I've told you I have nothing to do with them. If you choose not to believe me, that's your problem," she returned in a matter-of-fact tone as she stepped toward the center of the room.

"Yeah, right. Just a few minutes ago they were here at the door, sniffing around like hounds after a fox. How'd they find you so easily, Tasha, if you three aren't in cahoots?" He paced closer, then retreated. Tension wrinkled his face. She decided to ignore his last statement.

"Andrew, you need to relax. Sit down. I'll brew you some tea." She moved toward the bathroom, where there was a small coffeemaker she'd converted into her herbal tea maker.

As she passed Andrew, he reached out to grasp her arm. "I don't need any tea, Tasha. I need you to tell me what's going on here."

"I don't know, Andrew. What is going on here?" She whirled and faced him, only inches away, and spoke softly. His gaze penetrated hers for a few seconds. The dark navy flecks in his sky-blue eyes made her blood tingle. Where he touched her suddenly grew warm. After a moment, he gently released her arm and stepped away.

Tasha turned fully to watch him sit on the bed, rest his elbows on his knees, and lay his head in his palms. He sat there quietly for a moment. Silently, Tasha went about the task of brewing some tea—strong valerian tea. They both needed it.

Andrew looked up as she walked into the room, handed him a steaming cup of tea, and sat next to him on the bed. For a few minutes, they sipped their tea, avoiding looking at each other. When Andrew had drained his, Tasha took the mug from his hands and set both mugs on the bedside table.

"There now, isn't that better?" She turned, one leg tucked under her on the bed, and grasped his hands. He turned toward her and attempted a nod. Tasha had never a seen a more troubled man.

"All right. It doesn't do either of us any good to yell and be angry." She reached up and smoothed back a stray lock of hair on his forehead. "Obviously you've got some things on your mind that are making you quite upset. Can we talk about them calmly and maturely?"

Andrew sighed and glanced away, but she felt the clasp he had on her hands grow stronger. "I'm an idiot, Tasha. I need to apologize for the way I've been acting. Forgive me?" He glanced back to her face.

Tasha nodded. "I can and will forgive you, Andrew. But you need to explore where this anger came from. Will you talk about it with me?"

Andrew chuckled and Tasha was glad to hear it. It was the first sign he was relaxing. "Are you a shrink, too?"

She shook her head and smiled. "No. But I took some counseling classes while working on my undergraduate degree. I guess some of the stuff I learned rubbed off. Andrew, not to change the subject, but you need to talk about this."

"Now?"

"Is as good a time as any."

"I should just go home, Tasha. I should just go back to where I belong and forget this whole entire week. I'm a damned fish out of water here."

Tasha felt a wave of panic break through her. She didn't want him to leave. "Andrew, this is new to you—me, too—and it takes some adjustment. Those two guys threw a kink in the week.

Don't let that stop you from what you want to do. I mean, I know you're not into this whole free-spirit, anything-goes mentality, but we were having a pretty good start to the week and . . . oh, hell."

Andrew studied her for a minute. "Those two are up to something. It's driving me crazy. You're driving me crazy." He shook his head as if to shake away the direction of his thoughts.

Tasha waited. She didn't know what to say.

After a minute, he began again. "All right. I agree I need to hash this out. If you're willing to listen, then I'm ready to spill my guts."

"I'm an awfully good listener."

He nodded. "It's pretty simple. I'm a really good salesman and always have had top-notch sales figures. In fact, that's how I won this trip. There's a promotion coming up for someone in the firm soon, and I'm a likely candidate. However, Doug and Brett would both give their eyeteeth to get it. What I figure is this: They planned this whole trip, telling me it was a vacation spa, hoping they'd get me in some compromising position where they could blackmail me into resigning or get me fired. Either one would work for them."

"But how do you know this, Andrew? That's a pretty bizarre plan. To send you halfway across the world just to—"

"I wouldn't put anything past them. They want my job. They really want me out of the company."

Tasha thought for a minute. Strain was spreading across Andrew's face again. The stress was killing him.

"Is there anything else you want to say to me?"

He stared at her for a moment. Tasha could tell he was struggling internally. "Yes. I'm sorry I accused you of coming on to Doug. I guess . . . I was a bit—"

"Yes?" Tasha grinned slightly.

"All right, damn it! I was jealous, okay?"

A tingle welled up inside her at his admission. "Okay," she repeated softly and grinned shyly back. It had been a long time since anyone had admitted being jealous because of her, and it felt good.

But now that was out in the open, she wanted to get back to the most important thing at hand. If Andrew didn't come to terms with this thing with Doug and Brett and his job, the week would go downhill from now on.

"Andrew, about your job. Is it that important to you?"

As if in disbelief, he stared at her. "Yes," he answered bluntly.

"Why don't you quit it? Find another."

Andrew's eyes widened in surprise. "What? Quit? Why, there's too much at stake to quit."

"Like what?"

Andrew shook his head as if he couldn't comprehend what she had suggested. "Like my seniority. My pension plans. The stock I've bought in the company. The fringe benefits."

"The stress."

Andrew stared at her. "I could never quit my job."

"If you don't, you're going to have a heart attack before you're fifty."

He stood and shook his head. "No, I won't. I keep in good shape. I work out." He paced away.

"The stress will kill you, Andrew. It doesn't matter if you're in good shape. Look at you right now. I'll bet your blood pressure is sky high. You're anxious, your face is tense, you're pacing—"

Andrew stopped and faced her.

Tasha stepped closer and placed the palms of her hands on his shoulders. "And your muscles are tied up in knots." She squeezed and watched Andrew's eyes close with a small grimace at the pressure she'd placed on his shoulders. "You can't live like this, Andrew," she whispered. "No one can."

After a moment of massaging, she circled around to his back and began massaging his neck, shoulder, and back muscles. She led him back toward the bed. "Sit down. The least you can let me do is massage the kinks out. You'll feel a lot better in a few minutes."

For a while, Tasha knelt beside him on the bed, her fingers kneading. At first, Andrew sat stiff and erect, but after a few minutes of her tender assault, he let his shoulders drop and relaxed against her.

For the life of him, Andrew couldn't recall anything feeling so damned good for quite a long time. Tasha's fingertips were warm as they glided across his shirt and rubbed deep into his muscles. Closing his eyes, he let the sensation take him

CRAZY FOR YOU 105

away. He unbuttoned his shirt and slid it off his shoulders.

Tasha's fingers stopped as she touched his skin.

"Do you mind?" he asked softly. "Your fingers feel so good and I—"

"No," she replied quickly, a rasp in her voice. "I don't mind. Whatever works for you is fine with me," she added a little hesitantly.

Andrew let her continue in silence for several more minutes. After a while, he knew only the feel of the soft pads of her fingers relaxing his muscles and the drowsy, warm feeling in his head from her ministrations.

He was conscious of her even breathing behind him and the faint warmth of her breath against his heated skin. Deep inside, something broke loose and took hold. All too quickly, flames of desire leaped up and touched his heart. Before he realized it, he acted on that impulse and turned to face Tasha.

Her eyes were a dewy brown, wide and filled with questions. Her lips were full and plum red and moist. Her breathing had escalated into small pants; he could feel their moist warmth against his chest. Her hands had fallen to her lap as if she suddenly didn't know what to do with them.

Holding her gaze with his, Andrew reached out and cupped her cheek in his hand. As if drawn to him like a magnet, Tasha leaned forward to rest her face in his palm. Andrew captured her lips in a sweet embrace.

The kiss was gentle, soft, and lingering. Her lips were plump and inviting, and it was all Andrew could do to tear himself away from them. But he did.

He peered into her eyes for a moment longer and Tasha didn't move. Andrew realized how deeply they had been moved by the simple kiss. It scared the hell out of him.

He broke away and stood. While adjusting his shirt, he glanced down at Tasha. For a tall woman, she suddenly looked small and lost. Her face still held the questioning gaze it had moments earlier, before the kiss. It was as though she'd abruptly realized something, and it had taken her quite by surprise.

Well, he could understand that. He'd been taken by surprise himself.

SEVEN

"You need clothes."

Andrew looked at her as he buttoned his shirt. "Clothes?"

"You've worn those things for two days. Let's go shopping."

She turned away and stared out the window. Andrew could tell the subject of the kiss was taboo. Well, that was probably for the best. It wasn't something he wanted to discuss, either.

"Shopping."

"You know, you go into a store, pick out something you like, hand over money for it, and it's yours."

"I know what shopping is."

"Then let's do it. Shopping, I mean. Besides, you need something for this evening."

Andrew shook his head. The woman could certainly talk in circles. "What's going on this evening?"

"Well"—Tasha rose—"disco. The party starts at nine." She headed for the door. "Be there or be square. If your butt isn't there, I'll drag you there myself."

Andrew harbored no doubt she would.

She tossed him a threatening little smile and opened the door. "Coming?"

"Where?"

"Shopping."

He shook his head.

"Oh, pooh. Yes, you are."

"I don't do disco."

"No one *does* disco, Andrew. Disco just kind of does you." She smiled again and motioned with one finger for him to join her. "C'mon, let's try out those credit cards of yours."

"I'm not going shopping and I'm not doing disco."

With that smile on her lips as though she knew something Andrew didn't, she walked out the door, tossing her final words over her shoulder. "We'll see about that, Andrew Jacob Powell III."

The noise was deafening, the flashing lights blinding. There was even one of those gaudy rotating mirrored balls hanging from the ceiling. The bodies were crammed too close together, gyrating, giggling, spinning—some might even call it dancing. The room reeked of smoke and fruity alcohol drinks and K.C. and the Sunshine Band.

He hated smoke.

He hated fruity alcohol drinks.

He hated *disco*.

Why in hell was he here?

Andrew sauntered through the crowd to the bar at the back of the room. He tried to stay as inconspicuous as possible, but wondered how difficult that was going to be.

He had shopped that afternoon. Although he had difficulty finding exactly what he wanted, he'd come up with something close to his style. The trousers were more pleated than he would have liked, but they went with his wing tips. He had finally found a loud pair of deep purple socks that would suffice. He wouldn't be showing off his socks anyway.

The shirt was much too silky, had no collar, and was too snug, but it had a nice feel to it.

With his back to the bar, he eyed the crowd again.

He was way overdressed. Women with strapless and near-strapless mini-dresses did the bump and grind around the dance floor. Men with no shirts at all or with shirts open down to their navels followed them like sniffing hounds.

This was all ridiculous.

"Drink, sir?"

"Scotch," Andrew replied.

"With water?"

"Straight up." He needed a man's drink tonight. None of that fruity stuff for him.

"Coming right up."

Andrew eyed the dance floor. The mass of gyrating human flesh out there seemed to consist of nothing but legs and arms and a bobbing head once in a while, packed together like sardines. He had no clue how he would crowbar his way out of there. It appeared once one was claimed by that pulsating mass of flesh, one was consumed.

Not for him.

"Your drink, sir."

"Keep them coming."

"Yes, sir."

Andrew lifted the Scotch to his lips and let the liquid burn down this throat.

"Dance with me?"

The voice, a lilting southern drawl, came from his right. Slowly he turned to the woman, who stood not six inches away. He didn't need this, he thought, not another woman coming on to him and trying to—

Her hips swayed to the music in a slow, come-hither fashion, and suddenly Andrew was riveted to them. He followed the wiggle of her body up to her face. Her eyes were big and warm and brown and batted at him in a different come-hither way. Her lips were red and pouty and slightly parted.

He set his drink glass on the bar.

"Another one, sir?"

"Keep 'em coming."

"Yes, sir."

The southern belle inched forward.

Then he saw her, just behind the southern belle-slash-sex goddess. He didn't know how he'd missed her before now—tall, very tall, a head above everyone else, that mane of long brown hair swirling around her, and her legs. Oh, God. A black dress like that should be outlawed on a woman with legs that long. It barely covered her bottom, and there she was, turning and gyrating and shaking to "Shake Your Bootie."

"Want to dance?" the woman questioned again.

Andrew eyed the beauty before him, then glanced back at Tasha.

"I don't do disco," he said.

She sidled up a bit closer. "I can teach you. I can teach you lots."

I bet.

"Sorry. No." When was this kitten going to get the message?

"Andrew!"

From out of nowhere, Tasha emerged beside him. For the first time in two days, he was thankful. Grateful, even.

"Tasha!"

She rushed toward him, took his face between her two hands, and placed a hard little kiss right on his lips.

Momentarily, Andrew was frozen to the spot. No, welded to the spot. He couldn't move. All he could do was stare back into Tasha's eyes, which were laughing at him.

One glance to his right told him Miss Georgia Peach had split. Thank God.

"Thank you," he said to Tasha.

"What's the matter? Was she trying to put the moves on you?" She grinned, then turned to the bartender. "I'd like anything fruity," she told him. "Surprise me." Then, with another smile, she turned all of her attention back to Andrew.

"Dance with me?"

"I don't do disco."

"I can teach you."

Andrew swallowed. *I bet you could.*

Funny how these words from Tasha evoked all kinds of images the other woman's had not. What that meant, he wasn't sure—wasn't sure he liked it, either.

He downed his shot of Scotch, winced only slightly from the burn in his throat, and set the glass back down on the bar. Glancing to his left, he nodded to the bartender.

"Keep 'em coming?" the man asked.

"And how," Andrew replied.

Tasha watched Andrew throw back his third shot of Scotch in a few short minutes. At that rate, he wasn't going to last long. She needed to get him on the dance floor before he passed out.

"Come on, Andrew. Let's dance."

He held the empty glass in front of him like a shield. "I t-told you—"

"Oh, give it a rest."

Tasha took the glass out of his hand and set it on the bar with a thud. Then, taking his hands in hers, she slowly led him to the very center of the dance floor. He looked wonderful, she thought, having finally peeled himself out of that white dress shirt and navy pants. He'd taken her suggestion of shopping to heart and hadn't done a half bad job of it.

His eyes were riveted to her and she couldn't help but move provocatively, just a teeny bit, to the music.

He looked cute, so shy and insecure, as he allowed himself to be led into the throbbing masses—like a lamb being brought to slaughter, she thought, but that only amused her more. His eyes never left hers, and as she backed her way into the crowd, she ached to be closer to him.

"Know how to bump?" she asked.

Andrew glanced around. People were dancing and shouting and moving in circles around them. "Uh-uh."

"It's easy. Just stand there and watch me."

Tasha lifted her arms above her head and shifted to her left to bump hips with Andrew in time to the music. Then again.

He just watched.

"Think you got it?"

"That's it?"

"Well, that's my part," she replied. "You have to do the same thing on your end." She was shouting above the music now.

She bumped him again.

He just stood there.

Someone jostled her from behind, pushing her closer into Andrew. "You know," she said then, very close to his ear, "disco is like driving on the freeway. If you don't move with the flow of traffic, you're going to get run over. We either need to start moving so we don't get bumped into the floor, or we've got to get out of here."

"Oh." Andrew glanced from side to side.

"So which is it?"

He shook his head. Tasha thought he might be a little tipsy.

"Dance," he replied.

Smiling, Tasha nodded. "Go ahead. You can do it."

Lifting his arms slightly, he looked sheepishly at her and lightly touched his hip to hers.

Tasha laughed. "You can do better than that, can't you?"

Again, he lifted his arms and shifted to his right. Tasha bumped him back, nearly throwing him off balance into a woman dancing behind him. Quickly, he regained his balance.

"That wasn't fair. I wasn't ready."

Shaking her head, Tasha laughed again. "All right. Let's try something else." Stepping closer, she placed a hand on each of his hips. "Here, put your hands on my hips. Like what I'm doing."

Cautiously, narrowing his gaze and watching her intently, he did. Tasha stifled the grin that wanted to burst across her face.

"Move like this." She rotated her hips and shifted right, then left. "You've got to loosen up a bit. Unwind. Let—"

Suddenly, Andrew was pulling her closer. So close, in fact, paper wouldn't slide between them.

"Like this?" he whispered. His hands caressed her hips as he pulled her body into his. The beat of the song around them was fast, way too fast, Tasha thought, but they were finding a rhythm all their own.

"Yeah," she whispered back. "Like that."

In the next instant, the boogie beat fell away to a slow-moving ballad. The lights lowered and the crowd hushed.

Couples fell together, Andrew and Tasha among them.

Andrew's arms moved around her back and held her close. Her hands rose to his shoulders, and they swayed slowly together. His cheek rested against hers, the warm sweetness of his breath fanning out against her neck.

"See," he whispered after a moment. "I can dance."

Tasha closed her eyes and just let herself feel for a while. They moved together, swaying with the slow, sultry tune.

"Yes. Yes, you can," she whispered back. "And you do it very well."

Abruptly, the ballad halted and the pulsating lights started again. Reluctantly, it seemed, Andrew pulled away. Tasha was sorry to feel him leave her.

"I think I need to get out of here," he said.

Puzzled by the look on his face, Tasha asked, "Are you okay?"

"I don't know," he answered. As he stepped away, he stumbled and caught himself. "I think I'm about to get run over on the freeway."

Grinning, Tasha agreed. "Let me help you."

"I'm fine. Just need to—"

Someone slapped Andrew on the back. "Andrew, buddy! Into the disco scene, I see!"

Andrew's face curled into an expression of disgust—or maybe it was nausea. Tasha wondered if he'd eaten today. All that Scotch and an empty stomach might not fare too well.

"Doug. Fancy meeting you here."

The music kicked up its beat. Suddenly, Tasha felt herself grasped around the waist and pulled away into the crowd. When she finally had a chance to orient herself, she found she was looking into the face of Brett Southworth.

"What the hell are you doing?" she shouted at him.

He turned and danced in front of her, a provocative samba that was supposed to be sexy, she supposed.

"Dance with me, why don't you?"

"I don't want to." She turned and headed back toward Andrew.

He grasped her arm from behind.

She stopped. "What?"

"I said dance with me."

Glaring at him, she shook her head in disbelief. "Listen, buster, I don't know how you're used to treating women in Seattle, but that stuff doesn't work with me. Get your hand off me."

Brett grinned, and she hated that grin. Then he stepped back and let her go. "Hey, honey, didn't mean any harm. Go back to your boyfriend."

"He's not my boyfriend."

Brett cocked his head to one side. "Then dance with me."

"I don't dance with Neanderthals."

"Well, your boyfriend seems to be having a good time over there."

Glancing in the direction he was looking, Tasha picked Andrew out of the crowd. There he was, dancing with the bimbo who had tried to pick him up at the bar earlier.

She angled a glance back at Brett. "So how much did you pay her to dance with him? What have you got up your sleeve, you jerk?"

Brett looked straight ahead. "Didn't have to pay her a cent. Said she'd be glad to do it for free."

"I'll just bet," Tasha mumbled, making her way through the crowd.

A few seconds later, she tapped Miss Southern Hospitality on the shoulder. "My turn, sweetie. I'm cutting in."

"Tasha!"

"Hi, baby!"

Then she repeated what she'd done earlier to chase the bimbo away. She grabbed Andrew on either side of his face and kissed him. Right on the lips.

He tasted like Scotch and toothpaste.

Andrew wrapped his arms around her.

"I was dancing," he told her.

"I know."

"I was doing disco," he said.

"I know that, too."

"I'm drunk."

"Yes. You are. Let's go back to the room."

"I don't feel so good."

"Too much Scotch?"

"Too much disco," he answered.

And not enough dancing, Tasha thought to herself, *with me.*

***

Tasha watched Andrew sleeping in the roll-away bed across the room. His chest lifted with each breath he took, but his face occasionally grimaced, as if he were having a bad dream or unpleasant thoughts. She'd watched him for a long time.

Andrew hadn't been able to find his key, and Samuel was nowhere to be found. The door to his room was locked. Tasha did the next best thing and led Andrew back to her room, tucked him, clothes and all, into the roll-away, then settled in for the night herself.

Her sheet had slipped down to her waist, exposing her breasts. Andrew had fallen exhausted into bed as soon as they'd arrived in her room, and she'd decided to risk sleeping in the nude. It was hot, and she was uncomfortable. She'd be up before he was, anyway.

Her heart pounded in her chest as the cool night air breathed against her breasts, making them taut and firm and wanting. Maybe it wasn't the breeze at all. Maybe it was Andrew. Her mind recalled the feather touch of his fingers on her earlier while they were dancing.

What would it be like to make love to this left-brained Nordic god? He wasn't her type, was he? Then why was she all of a sudden—well, all right, she'd been chewing this over for a while—thinking of having sex with him?

Would it be just sex?

The feelings he evoked inside her sure felt like a whole lot more than that.

For two days now, she'd wondered exactly why

she felt she needed to stay close to Andrew. Was it because he challenged her and she wanted to see him do something totally uncharacteristic? Was it because she wanted him to loosen up a bit and dump some of the conservative attitudes? Or was it because she wanted *him*, period?

But once she had him, what was she going to do with him? Keep him like a little lost puppy she'd saved from the hands of the dogcatcher? Her mother always said she had to have a cause, a project going. So far she'd helped save whales, bats, snail darters, pandas, pregnant teenagers, the homeless, and taught organic farming on an Indian reservation. Was Andrew her next cause? Save the Yellow-Crested-Stuffed-Shirt from a life of boredom?

She wasn't after commitment, not at this point in her life. She'd just dumped Mark, and commitment had been her biggest problem. She'd wanted a relationship with him, but didn't know if she wanted to commit to what he wanted of her for the rest of her life. She valued Mark for what he was—her friend. She didn't want to ruin that with the commitment of marriage. Free spirits didn't like commitments, and she was a free spirit. Wasn't she? She'd had too much of the bohemian lifestyle drilled into her to deny it.

So what the hell did she want here?

Why didn't she want to let Andrew Jacob Powell III go his merry way back to his mundane life in Seattle?

EIGHT

"Okay, up and at 'em, big boy. It's time to get going!"

Andrew lifted one eyelid and squinted at Tasha. "Are you referring to my stature in general or to a certain part of my anatomy?" he growled, then turned away from her, jerking the sheets up to his neck, afraid to know the answer.

"Just a statement in general. C'mon, get up. We've got places to go, things to do." She jerked on the sheets.

"Go away. This is my vacation. I want to sleep in."

"Party pooper." She slapped him on the rear. "C'mon. There's not much of a crowd out there. A big group is going off the resort to some sort of mass snorkeling adventure today, so there won't be oodles of people ogling us. Let's head to the beach and check it out. Want to?"

Andrew pulled down the sheet a bit and rolled over. He was half afraid to approach this beach subject with her. "Don't you ever shut up and listen? Read my lips: I—want—to—sleep—in."

Ignoring him, she whisked the sheet away from the bed.

CRAZY FOR YOU 121

Andrew bolted upright and snatched it back to his body, but not before Tasha had gotten a good glimpse of him. He'd stripped sometime during the night; the heat was unbearable.

"Uh, maybe I was referring to your anatomy," she mumbled and walked away. "Since you're already nude, let's just go. But you'll have to wear something between here and there." She started unfastening the buttons of her chambray shirt.

Standing at the side of the bed, Andrew held out one hand and attempted to wrap the sheet around his waist with the other. "Wait! What are you doing?"

Tasha already had the buttons undone down to her denim shorts and was ready to tug the bottom out of the waistband. "I'm changing into my swimsuit until we get to the beach. Look, it's now or never. Are you coming or not?"

Andrew contemplated the question.

"Tasha, look, I don't think I ought to try out that nude beach right now, you know? With Doug and Brett out there somewhere waiting to get a snapshot of me . . . well, it could be humiliating when I get back to the office."

"Oh, didn't I tell you?" Tasha stepped closer and tugged at his sheet. Her shirt fell open a bit. *Oh, God.* "I was up early this morning meditating with Samuel."

Andrew threw her a curious look.

"He told me Doug and Brett got thrown out of the resort after the disco party last night. Evidently they got rowdy and out of hand in one of the nude Jacuzzis. They had a camera, which is strictly against regulations in that area of the resort. They were taking pictures of the nude guests. One of them got irritated and reported it to the management. They ousted both of them like hot potatoes and escorted them back to the airport. So . . . since they're gone, you have nothing to worry about." Tasha smiled and Andrew felt his face fall.

"Well?" she probed.

He stared at her. "They got back to the airport?"

Tasha frowned. "Hmmm . . . appears so. I'm sure management has a vehicle around here somewhere for emergencies. And I'm sure, Andrew, *your* situation would not be considered an emergency. What would you tell them? That the excitement was getting to you?"

He eyed her. "You're impossible."

Switching the subject back to the beach, Tasha asked, "So are you coming with me or not?"

"All right, I'm coming. Just give me a minute to get dressed." Somehow he didn't like the thought of her going there alone, even though he didn't want to go there himself.

"Well, you don't have to do anything special on my account. Just put on your swim trunks and let's get going." She lowered the shirt over her shoulders as she stepped toward the door, her back to him. Andrew watched the blue fabric slowly drop to the floor, revealing her back. Her smooth, lightly tanned back. Soft shoulders. Narrow waist.

This woman is driving me insane.

"I've got to brush my teeth."

"So brush them. I'll wait."

"My stuff is in Samuel's room."

"So go get your stuff and meet me back here."

"No, you go on. I'll catch up."

"Like hell. We do this together."

"I . . . I've changed my mind. Actually, I don't think I ever decided. I think you decided for me."

Turning, she faced him. "No," she said through gritted teeth, "you have not changed your mind."

"I have." *Man, did she look good.*

"What's the matter, afraid you won't measure up? Is that it? Are you embarrassed, Mr. Stuffed Shirt?"

When she looked at him like that, her nostrils flared, her hair all fanned out over her bare shoulders, her long, barely clad legs spread apart in a stance that said she meant business, Andrew knew he'd gone too far. He couldn't back out now.

He took one step toward the door. Inside, his stomach jerked and flinched. He took another step. Something in his chest quivered. His throat constricted. He didn't think he could breathe.

I can't do this.

"Look. I promise I'll meet you at the beach, okay? Just let me go back to my room and clean up a bit." He turned to gather his clothes. "In fact, why don't you go on so I can get dressed to go back to my room? I promise I'll find you."

"Andrew, this is bunk. You're not going and we both know it."

". . . I have every intention—"

"Well, I'm not waiting for you. I'll be at the beach—if you decide to come—having the time of my life. You, on the other hand, will be pining away for the safety and security of Seattle. So you know what? Go for it. I, for one, do not plan to waste another minute. *Ciao*, baby."

She turned and walked straight out the door without a towel, without her shoes, without anything other than her bikini top and her denim shorts.

Andrew didn't like watching her walking away from him.

The note on his bed read simply:

Toga party tonight. Be there or be square.

He didn't have to wonder who it came from. Samuel wasn't into parties, he'd told Andrew. They messed up his concentration too much for meditation. The note most definitely was from Tasha.

After returning to his room that morning—luckily finding Samuel there, because he still hadn't located his key—he'd donned a pair of shorts and a polo-type shirt he'd bought the day before. He should have bought some sort of shoes, but hadn't. He decided to be wild and crazy like everyone else around here and go barefoot.

Score one for the businessman.

It felt extremely uncomfortable, but was infinitely better than wearing his purple socks and wingtips.

He'd walked around most of the morning and afternoon. He did wide circles around the nude beach area. He didn't care if Tasha was there, he wasn't going to go there. No matter what he'd told her.

He checked out the *normal* beach for *normal* people and wished for once Tasha was a *normal* person. Those people were having fun out there. They saw no need to be exhibitionists, shed their clothes, and parade around in their birthday suits. They were out enjoying the sun and the surf and having a good time in the process.

Why couldn't that be Tasha and him?

Because Tasha wasn't a *normal* person. And if the truth were known, that was the attraction.

Of course, Andrew didn't want to admit that to himself.

Throughout the day, he'd checked out every nook and cranny: the bars (one complete with piano), the circus workshop, the snorkeling and scuba diving lessons (he just watched), the windsurfing school, the tennis courts, the fitness club, the volleyball courts (there was a nude one of those, too, he found out), the dining hall (he had lunch), and even a library. That was enough excitement for him throughout the day.

But it was the people who amazed him.

They flitted from one activity to another, scantily clad, with ecstatic smiles on their faces.

They were happy. Carefree. Nary a worry in the world.

Andrew sat on the side of his bed and glanced across the room to view himself in the mirror. And there the tale was told:

There was a scowl on his face.

He wasn't scantily clad.

He wasn't carefree.

He carried the worries of the world on his shoulders.

Looking again at the note in his hand, he thought once more, long and hard, about the coming evening.

In the next instant he ripped the sheet from his bed and went in search of Samuel. "If anyone knows how to make a toga out of one of these things, he should," Andrew mumbled to himself.

With that, he decided to become, or at least attempt to become, somewhat . . . uninhibited.

Tasha fiddled with the toga strap that ran over her left shoulder, around her back, and then tied at her waist. *The darned thing,* she thought. *How in the world am I ever going to keep this stupid sheet intact?*

She should have used safety-pins, but she'd had none and couldn't find any in the small shop off the hotel lobby.

It was only a twin sheet. Her king-size sheet was way too big, so she'd swiped the one off the roll-away. With her height, it made the toga rather skimpy, and she hadn't worn underwear. Oh, geez. Maybe she shouldn't dance too much.

She figured Andrew would never know the difference about the sheet. Most likely he wouldn't share her room again anyway. She hadn't seen hide nor hair of him since that morning.

She'd known he wouldn't show up at the beach. That was predictable. She just thought somehow, for some reason, he would have contacted her later in the day, especially since he knew what was on the agenda tonight. She'd managed to have Samuel sneak the note onto Andrew's bed. However, that didn't mean he would show up. In fact, if he *did* show up here, she'd probably have to—

"Well I'll be damned," she whispered to herself.

There he was, in head-to-toe toga.

A lazy smile stretched across her face. He looked damned cute in a toga.

She watched as he headed straight toward the bar he'd frequented the night before. She had already figured, as a creature of habit, he would do just that. And there she was, waiting for him, his Scotch in one hand and her fruity umbrella drink in the other.

His gaze shifted from side to side and Tasha knew he was trying not to call attention to himself or show his discomfort with the entire situation.

The people around them reveled. At the moment, drinking and dancing and eating were the only things on the card. However, she knew for a fact things were going to get quite a bit more interesting before the night was through.

That was why she had Andrew's Scotch in hand.

He was almost directly in front of her before he stopped long enough to realize Tasha was standing before him. He gulped, and his eyes grew wide as they trailed down and back up her body.

"Drink, sailor?" Tasha pushed the Scotch his way.

He took the glass, downed the amber liquid posthaste, and returned it. In turn, Tasha set the glass on the bar and nodded to the bartender.

"He'll keep them coming." She winked at Andrew.

"Good."

Tasha laughed.

After a moment, he sighed and his shoulders relaxed. Then he slid up next to her, leaning against the bar. "I feel ridiculous."

"You look peachy."

"Peachy?"

"Ummm . . . good enough to eat."

"What?" Andrew stepped back. Tasha sidled next to him again.

"Don't worry, Andrew. I won't bite you—not yet, at least."

He gulped again and reached for his second shot. "That's what I'm afraid of," he mumbled into the glass.

Grinning, Tasha pushed away from the bar. "Oh, look! It's time for the toga fashion review!" She grabbed Andrew's hand and started for the center of the floor.

Andrew had no choice but to follow. "Toga fashion review?"

"Yes, I hope you don't mind. I signed us up."

Andrew stopped cold in the center of the floor, dragging Tasha to a halt with him. "You did *what*?"

"I signed us up! This will be so cool. Just you wait and see."

Andrew took three steps backward. "Uh-uh. No. You're out of your fruity little head."

She turned and headed for a makeshift runway, dragging him behind her. "C'mon, this will be a piece of cake. All you have to do is walk down this runway. Oh, look! It's starting."

"Sure. Fun."

"We have to hurry. We're numbers three and four."

Stopping, she slapped a large number three on his chest and a number four on her hip. "Let's go!"

She led him to the stairway at the left of the stage. Before he knew it, she was pushing him up the stairs and onto the stage.

He stopped, stone cold frozen, right in the center of the stage. Stage fright, he thought they called it. There was no way he was moving.

A thousand hands and arms were waving and swaying and grabbing at the two contestants before him as they made their way down the runway—grabbing at their legs, at their togas. Oh, god. What if—

And they were shouting rude, crude things.

Sexual things like "ooh baby" and "hubba hubba."

"Andrew, move!"

It was Tasha, yelling at him. Telling him to go.

Then she was at his side, hooking her arm with his and pulling him down the runway.

"Lighten up, Andrew. Relax! It's all in good fun!" she yelled out over the music and the chanting crowd.

Someone touched the calf of his leg. He jumped. "Oooh . . . baby! I want you!" some deranged woman called out.

"No, he's mine!" another woman cried.

"Kaaaarrummmba!" Another female voice screamed. "The blond is mine!"

Andrew threw a shocked glance at Tasha. She tossed back her head and laughed. She was in her element, sashaying down the runway. He, on the other hand, had had enough. She must have sensed that, for she quickly turned and led him back up the runway and down the steps.

At the bottom of the stairs, he turned on her. "You are absolutely nuts!"

"Yes, probably." She grinned.

"That was the most humiliating thing that has *ever* happened to me in my entire life!"

Laughing now, Tasha replied, "Oh, goody, and I'm the responsible party. Did it feel good, Andrew?" She was still laughing.

Shaking his head, he glared at her. "I don't get it. Why do you want to humiliate me? What's the deal, Tasha?"

Her face turned more serious then. "I don't

want to humiliate you, Andrew. I just want to see you loosen up, have fun, relax. That's all I'm after. Chill out, why don't you?"

And then she turned and walked away. Again.

The next afternoon, Andrew returned to his room after his customary walk around the resort. The note on his bed this time read:

Karaoke night. Nine o'clock. Bayside Bar. Be there or be square.

This was where he drew the line. He'd endured her anger about the nude beach thing, he'd suffered through disco, he'd survived the toga incident.

But there was no way, no cotton-picking way, she was going to get him to a karaoke bar.

Absolutely no way.

It was impossible.

The singing coming from the open air bar was off-key and made his teeth tingle.

Andrew had no idea what he was doing here. In fact, he figured he was just one big glutton for punishment.

Truth was, however, he couldn't fathom the idea of sitting in the hotel room he shared with Samuel tonight while the rest of Jamaica was out having a good time.

And while Tasha was out having a good time with Jamaica without him.

He figured at the very least this would be an opportunity to see her. He was pretty darned safe. No one anywhere could force him to sing karaoke. If they did, they'd be mighty sorry.

He stepped up to the bar and grimaced as a woman with curly black hair tried to make her way through a rendition of some Whitney Houston song.

He was terrible with titles, yet he recognized the tune somewhat, as one he'd liked in the past. This woman was butchering the thing.

"Scotch, sir?"

Andrew glanced to the bartender. The man showed a toothy grin. Smiling back in recognition, Andrew nodded.

"Straight up."

"And keep them coming?"

"Damned straight.

The bartender slid the drink close to the edge of the bar. Andrew grasped the glass, threw back the drink, and sighed long and easy at the welcome, warm thud in his stomach.

He was becoming way too accustomed to his Scotch.

Scanning the room, he looked for signs of Tasha but found none. There wasn't a huge crowd; this bar was smaller, away from the hotel and closer to the beach. Surely he was at the right place.

He glanced over his shoulder. "What's the name of this bar?" he asked the bartender.

"Bayside, sir."

"Then this is the one."

"Yes, sir. Looking for the tall brunette?"

Andrew faced him fully. "Have you seen her?"

"Oh, yes, mon. Earlier." He pushed another shot glass toward Andrew. "Best to drink up. Never know what a woman has in her head."

Andrew chuckled and downed the drink. "You got that right, mister."

He looked back at the stage in time to see the black-haired woman leave. The crowd snickered and booed her all the way.

"Terrible what people will do for attention," he muttered.

"Yes, sir." Another Scotch came his way.

"Can't believe anyone would get up there and make an idiot out of himself like that. Floors me."

"See it all the time, mon."

Andrew kicked back his third Scotch.

"Might want to slow down a bit on those, sir."

Andrew waved the guy off. "Ah, hell! I can handle my Scotch. None of those tutti-frutti drinks for this guy. Besides"—he passed the glass back to the bartender—"I'm not driving. Can you get arrested for drunk walking?"

Andrew chuckled at his own humor, and the man behind the bar chuckled with him. "No, sir. One cannot."

"Another, my good man."

"Coming right up."

Within the next few minutes, he downed his fourth Scotch. By that time, the woman on the stage announcing the karaoke contestants looked a mite fuzzy but sounded too much like someone he knew. Probably someone from back in Seattle, he thought. Probably someone—

"And for our next contestant," her voice boomed out over the bar, "we have a very special treat. All the way from Seattle, let's give a big round of applause to Mr. Andrew Jacob Powell III!"

He squinted and looked again at the woman behind the mike. It was . . . wasn't it?

Every face in the house was turned his way.

"It's your turn, sir."

Glancing back to the bartender, he asked, "It's her, isn't it?"

"Afraid so, mon. Afraid so."

"I'm drunk."

"It will make you sing a whole lot better."

Andrew squinted at the man and agreed. "I think you're right. Lemme at 'em."

The last thing he remembered was belting out "Hey Jude" and then "The Lion Sleeps Tonight" followed by a sappy rendition of "You've Got a Friend." He was trying to sing "Desperado," when Tasha finally dragged him off the stage and pointed him back toward his hotel room.

He couldn't remember if she or Samuel tucked him into bed, but he was mighty glad to be there.

NINE

Sometime in the night, Tasha decided the best thing she could do for herself and for Mr. Andrew Jacob Powell III was to ignore him, to pretend he didn't exist, not acknowledge his presence, aggravate him, or make her presence or her views known to him at all—do nothing, nada, nil, zilch.

She was her own woman now. As her own woman, she would do whatever she pleased the remainder of her vacation without one conservative, Nordic-god-of-a-Republican businessman putting in his two cents' worth.

She rather liked the independence of it all.

For the first time all week, she was glad she wasn't going to have to be concerned with Andrew any longer.

She'd felt bad last night after she'd tucked him into bed. The man had resorted to drinking the past three nights because of her, and she didn't know if she wanted that on her conscience for the rest of her life.

And she had been purposely humiliating him. Well, not purposely. Those things just sort of happened. How was she to know it would be difficult to peel Andrew off the stage after he'd had a few?

No one could have predicted that.

So it was for the best if she kept her distance for a while, did her own thing, and let him do his own thing.

As she walked down the trail toward the volleyball courts, she contemplated her newly found freedom.

I mean, really, Tasha, she told herself. *You came down here to get over the funk you were in about Mark. Then, like an idiot, you attach yourself to this man who has definite problems in the free-spirit category. Jeez. You couldn't have picked a more unlikely candidate to get to know on this trip if you'd advertised for a suit in the personals.*

She followed the trail into a forested area, complete with palms and foliage, huge tropical flowers, and now and then a hammock built for two. Every once in awhile, she had to turn her head away from those hammocks, particularly the ones occupied with sleeping lovers beneath a blanket.

Why couldn't I have hooked up with some free spirit who'd want to cuddle under a blanket out in the woods? Instead, she had attached herself to Andrew Powell.

Thing was, she liked being attached to Andrew . . .

"I've got a problem," someone said.

"You're not the only one, buddy," Tasha muttered.

Abruptly, she halted and looked up. Andrew was standing directly in front of her. "Oh! Andrew, it's you!"

He tossed her a puzzled look. "Who did you think it was?"

"I-I didn't know. I was lost in thought. I was thinking about . . . well, I suppose you wouldn't want to know what I was thinking about."

"Try me."

"Uh-uh."

"Whatsamatter, you chicken?"

Tasha suddenly felt like the tables had been turned on her. "Chicken? Me? You jest, sir."

"What were you thinking?"

She studied him for a second, then decided to go for it.

"Sex," she blurted out. "I was thinking of sex."

They both stood there, awkwardly glancing about and shuffling their feet, each obviously trying to figure out what the next move was.

Tasha cleared her throat. *Okay,* she told herself. *Get a grip.* "You said you had a problem?"

"Yes. A dilemma."

"And are you going to tell me about this dilemma?"

Again, Andrew glanced about, shoved his hands deep into the pockets of his shorts, cleared his throat, and shifted from one foot to another.

"I lost my room."

"How does one lose a room?"

"Samantha has arrived."

Tasha arched a brow. "Samantha?"

He nodded. "Samuel's sister. She's visiting from Minneapolis. Guess she divides her time between both places. At any rate, she arrived this morning and I got the boot."

Tasha slowly dropped her chin in a nod. "Ah. And now you're stuck. No place to stay."

"Precisely."

"And you were thinking?"

"I was thinking you might consider, um, sharing that roll-away . . . I mean, er, not sharing the roll-away, but sharing the room. I mean, of course, you can have the king and I can have the roll-away and we'd have to work out things like sharing the bathroom and such, but we only have a few more days, and the bus strike isn't over yet because I checked at the desk, and I thought—"

Tasha put up a hand. "Stop. Take a breath. That is the longest sentence I've heard in my entire life."

"So what do you think?"

She eyed him and he squirmed. Why did she like watching him squirm? She didn't know.

"I'm not sure it's a good idea."

"Why?"

"Because of sex."

"Sex?"

"The thing two people do when—"

This time Andrew put up his hand. "I know what sex is. Believe me."

Sighing, Tasha crossed her hands over her chest and shifted one hip out to the side. She waited for several minutes, watching him, then said, "I suppose you could sleep in the roll-away."

Andrew closed his eyes. "Thank you."

"You're welcome."

"Are you heading back to the room?" he asked

Shaking her head, she returned, "No, actually

CRAZY FOR YOU

I was heading down the hill to the volleyball court." She reached into her pocket, pulled out her room key, and handed it to him. "But here. Go get your stuff and put it in my room. If you need to leave before I get back, leave the key at the desk. I'll get another one for you later."

She turned and started walking away, sensing Andrew watching her.

"Where did you say you're going?" he asked again.

"Volleyball," she tossed over her shoulder and kept walking.

Volleyball.

Andrew watched her walk away. Then he glanced to his right at the signs pointing out the directions to several of the activity areas. He did a doubletake.

"Hey! Come back here!"

She stopped and turned to look at him.

"You're going the wrong way," he told her.

Tasha looked back down the hill, then up to him again. "No, I'm going the right way."

"No, I'm sure you're not. That's the way to the nude volleyball court."

Tasha grinned. "Precisely." She turned and headed back down the hill.

Whoa, Andrew. Stop. Don't go there. It's none of your business.

He tried to control himself—tried like hell to control himself. But he couldn't.

"Wanna join me?" Tasha was beckoning and smiling. Wickedly.

"Who, me?"

"Yes, you, silly. Come on!"

For one second, he seriously considered it. He even took a half step forward.

Then his throat constricted, his stomach did a wallop, and his heart beat out a strange tattoo.

"No, sorry. Can't do it."

Tasha shrugged. "Okay, no biggie. I guess I can't force you."

"That's right."

"But it sure doesn't mean I can't do it."

She sashayed off down the path.

"Tasha!" he called out after her. "Wait! Don't." Suddenly, the notion of her parading around naked in front of strangers didn't sit well with him. He didn't mind, of course, if she wanted to parade around in front of *him*. That was another thing altogether. But strangers?

She stopped in her tracks and threw a look over her shoulder. "What do you want? There's a volleyball game down there I intend to get in on."

He stood there, watching her standing among the trees and plants like she belonged there. She was tempting him, yes. Could he play Adam to her Eve? She was an incredible creature, a wood nymph. An overgrown one, but a wood nymph just the same. She belonged there.

He didn't.

"I don't want you to do this," he whispered, surprised he'd even said the words.

Her body jerked a bit and he thought she would come to him, but she didn't. After a moment, she backed up half a step. "Sorry," she whispered back, "but I make my own decisions. And I don't go back on them."

She turned and sauntered off down the path. Andrew's heart sank to the pit of his stomach.

Lying on the roll-away, the sheet draped over his waist, Andrew was thinking—thinking about this damned predicament he'd gotten himself into. Less than a week ago, he'd been making his rounds, keeping up his quota, riding around in his suit and his air-conditioned car.

Now, he was lying on a bed in a strange woman's hotel room somewhere in Jamaica. Crazy. The whole damned world had gone crazy.

She was down there playing volleyball. And he was thinking about that real hard, how she was down there somewhere, naked among the masses, also naked, doing God-knows-what naked. He hated it.

Andrew sat up. His stomach spasmed in several quick thrusts, tightening and gripping. *Nerves,* he told himself. *That's all.* He was nervous about this whole situation. Nervous about her down there alone, naked, jumping around playing volleyball. Oh, God.

He jumped up off the bed.

Hell, who was he kidding? He didn't want her down there doing God-knows-what. He wanted her here with him.

Naked.

Oh, all right! He'd admit it! He wanted her

under him, over him—he didn't care. And he didn't feel like sharing.

He waited about three minutes more, then left the room. It was all he could stand.

Andrew stomped off down the path toward the volleyball game. From his hiding place behind a large palm, he thought he saw her. He'd been thinking about her for the past few minutes, what she would look like down there playing volleyball. He could just imagine the little sybarite jumping up and down, anticipating the ball coming to her, her perfectly shaped breasts jiggling—nice and firm, not droopy—and her buns, nicely shaped, fully packed, probably with cute little dimples on either side of her backbone right above them. The palms of his hands ached. Damn. He wanted to touch her. He wanted to touch her now.

And he didn't want anyone else ogling her.

There wasn't another woman anywhere who could compare with her.

But she might be ogling other men.

"Probably getting an eyeful, aren't you, Tasha," he muttered disgustedly as he caught sight of the game in progress. "You should be ashamed."

He stepped a little closer, weaving his way through the trees. He'd stepped off the beaten path so as not to be noticed.

A shriek went up and Andrew's attention was immediately drawn back to the game. A muscled man beside Tasha jumped up and into her body, knocking her down to the ground.

"Aw, hell . . ." Andrew ran down the path.

"Andrew! Where are you going?"

CRAZY FOR YOU

Startled, he stopped abruptly and turned. Tasha? Another screech bounced through the trees. He jerked his head back toward the volleyball game. Or was that Tasha down there?

"Andrew!" Again he turned abruptly back to the sound of the voice. Tasha stepped out from behind a tree.

"What are you doing down here?"

He turned fully to face her, a bit confused. He parked his fists on his hips. "I thought you were down there playing volleyball," he barked back at her.

Tasha angled her gaze at him. "I changed my mind. Why were you heading that way?"

Andrew started to glance behind him. "I thought," he began, and then hesitated. "Hell, I thought you were down there. I didn't want you down there. And then I heard this scream and I thought it was you."

"So you were going after me?"

"I was gonna drag your butt back up to the room if I had to." Andrew clamped his mouth shut and firmed his stance in front of her. His words surprised even him.

Tasha threw back her head and laughed. "Oh, you were, were you? May I ask if you were going to knock me over the head with a bone and drag me back by my hair?"

"I was going to tell you to get your little bottom back up to the hotel where it belonged. In fact, that's exactly what I think you should do right now. Do you understand me?"

Tasha's eyes widened. She slanted her gaze at him. "Come again?"

His hands hit his hips in desperation. "I said hightail your fanny back up that hill where you belong. Now."

Calmly, Tasha stepped away from him. "I don't think so." She brushed past him, heading for the game.

"Tasha!" He rushed up next to her. "You're going to hear me out, you understand me? I want you back at the room, now."

"Leave me alone."

Anger welled up inside his chest. He looked down at the fists at his sides, clenching and unclenching uncontrollably. "No, I will not leave you alone. I will not allow you to go down there and play volleyball with naked people. What are you, some kind of exhibitionist?"

Silence rang out through the woods. Tasha slowly angled her gaze back to him.

"I think you'd better leave me alone, Andrew. You're walking on thin ice. You have nothing to say about what I do or where I go. In fact, I think *you'd* better go back to the room now."

"Not without you."

"Why?"

"Because—" Suddenly all the fight went out of him. "Oh, hell, forget it, Tasha. I don't know why I'm doing this. You're right. It's your decision. Come back whenever you're ready." Andrew tore his gaze away from her face and started walking back up the hill toward the hotel.

"You could take off your clothes and join me," she called out after him.

Andrew ignored her.

"Don't you walk away from me, Andrew Jacob Powell! I'm not finished with you yet, you conservative little jackass!"

Tasha burst through the hotel room door, her gaze riveted on Andrew standing across the room. Of all the unmitigated gall.

"Who the hell do you think you are?"

Andrew dragged his hands over his face, then sat down on the rattan chair. "Tasha, look, I'm sorry. I don't know what came over me. It's just that I didn't—"

"Yeah! That's right, you didn't think. Period." As she reached him, she planted both hands firmly on either arm of Andrew's chair and looked him square in the eyes. "Let me tell you something, Mr. Conservative. It's my life, my body, my vacation, and I'll do as I damned well please." She poked him in the chest, punctuating each word. "And you'd better remember that."

She kept her gaze locked with his for a moment. He shifted slightly in his seat, adjusting the direction of his gaze—which was quite a bit lower than her chin. In fact, he was staring directly at her chest. The look on his face was one of pure lust.

Or was it? God, she hoped it was lust. She couldn't handle anything other than lust right now, especially feelings. Emotions.

Tasha jerked back and stood to her full height, her hands automatically resting on her hips. Suddenly, she felt flushed. Her cheeks were hot and she bet if she looked down, her breasts would be blushing. She didn't look down. She didn't want to know. "Seen enough?" she taunted.

"Yes." She could tell he was lying.

"Good." Tasha turned and made her way across the room, dodging the crumpled sheet on the floor.

"Tasha . . ." Andrew's voice was hoarse.

She turned to stare at him. "What?"

"I didn't want you to get hurt," he said quietly, his gaze touching hers and holding. He still sat in the chair, unmoving. "I didn't want you to get in over your head. I didn't want anyone else seeing you, watching you . . . touching you," he admitted.

Turning fully to him, Tasha took one step forward. "What?" she asked again, quietly this time, her eyebrows knit in the center.

"I was afraid of what would happen. That you'd get down there with that"—he swallowed—"with that drop-dead gorgeous body of yours, and someone . . . some pervert or some macho man would sweep you off your feet and carry you away and I'd never see you again."

Andrew gritted his teeth. Where was all this coming from? Why was he telling her this? Was this truly how he felt, or was he just making all this up to look good in her eyes?

No, he wasn't making it all up. Suddenly, he recognized his fears, and they weren't about getting naked. His fears had a whole lot more to do with her body than his. How he wanted that body—and not just for the week.

Oh, God, he realized. *I care for her.*

Tasha took another two steps forward. "And that would bother you?"

He nodded. "Uh, yeah. It would bother me a lot."

Andrew searched her eyes for . . . anything, anything at all that would tell him how she was feeling. He'd finally put his finger on the emotion he'd felt earlier when she'd left him. He'd felt desperate and helpless. Those feelings were racing across him now. As far as Tasha was concerned, he'd fallen into a chasm of desperate helplessness and didn't have a clue as to how to dig his way out.

It had shaken the hell out of him to think about her naked with other people, even if it was only during a volleyball game.

"But I don't want it to bother you!"

Her statement was bold, blunt, loud, and to the point. Tasha's eyes went wild with unexpected fury. "I don't want it to bother you one damned bit! Do you understand?"

She moved to the center of the room, gathering some of her things into her arms, and tossed a troubled glance back at him.

"This is a vacation, Andrew. One week out of one year out of hundreds of years out of millennia. It doesn't amount to squat. It's not real. And what happens here, whatever that might be, won't leave here. Do you understand that? At the risk of sounding hokey, you and I aren't beans. We don't matter to each other now and we won't when we leave. This is fiction. Fantasy. And whether or not you ever take off your clothes, whether or not we play naked volleyball or tennis or bingo together, or even if we make love, for that matter, it's not real. We're floating above whatever we deem normal in some vision of what we might hope or dream. This"—she swept her arms about her—"is Fantasy Island. But after we leave here, there won't be any reruns."

Andrew narrowed his eyes at her in disbelief and pain wrenched through his gut. "You're sure about that?"

Tasha nodded her head once in acknowledgment. "Whatever happens to us or between us for the next few days doesn't exist when we leave this place. It's for the best for you, for me, for everyone. We're too far apart. Nothing alike. You know that; so do I. There could never be anything more." And with that, she left him alone and bewildered, especially at the small tear that had slipped over her lower eyelid just before she'd left.

TEN

It stormed during the night, a powerful storm that forced them to shut the windows and brave the unbearable heat. Then the rain passed and the power failed, leaving them with high humidity and no chance of air conditioning for several days to come, they were told.

But Tasha wasn't going to let it get her down. She still had two days and she intended to make the most of them.

She had studied a map of the grounds the day before. Approximately a mile off the beaten path to the north of the hotel was a small, man-made lake, complete with waterfall. When she'd called to inquire, Todd told her it was fairly secluded and safe for swimming. Most people preferred the pool or the beach and didn't bother with the lake. However, some preferred the privacy the lake offered.

It was just what she was looking for. The temperature had spiked to ninety-plus degrees. The surrounding rain forest reeked with humidity, the bugs were invading, and she was going to have to get Andrew out of that hotel room soon or they would both go absolutely loony-tunes, especially after yesterday.

She was drained emotionally. All night long, she'd thought about what she'd said to Andrew, how he'd looked at her, and how her heart had plunged to her feet when she'd walked out on him.

Andrew Jacob Powell III cared for *her*? Well, she couldn't let it go any further. She liked being with Andrew, yes, and this challenge she'd thrown up to herself about loosening the man up a bit had been fun. But caring? Affection? Did she really want that?

No emotions, Tasha. Remember? You don't do well with emotions.

But she couldn't stop thinking about Andrew. Never in her life had she been involved in a relationship so volatile, and yet so satisfying. Was that good or bad? She actually enjoyed sparring with him. They sparked off each other, which made things more intense. Then the emotional factor started getting in the way.

Her little speech yesterday was the best thing that could have happened. It let them both off the hook, gave them an out. They each knew a relationship between them would never work. They were total opposites, for heaven's sake! She was just glad she'd had enough guts to lay it all out on the line.

It had been late when she'd returned to the room. Andrew was fast asleep—or feigning sleep very well. She wasn't sure which.

She'd risen early and conned Josh into letting her pilfer some groceries from the kitchen. He had obliged wholeheartedly. She was going to have to get Andrew out of that room, and if presenting him with a peace offering of a picnic by the lake would do it, then she'd just have to suck up her pride.

Her arms laden with four grocery bags, she rapped on the room door. After a minute, a sleepy-eyed Andrew answered.

"Becoming a late sleeper these days?"

Tasha brushed past him, trying to forget how he'd made her feel, but the sensations came zinging back at her. She tried to forget about the burning, wanting imprint he'd left on her after the dance the other night, tried to forget she'd lain awake half the night for the past two nights wondering just what made Andrew Powell tick and why she sparked off him. All her earlier convictions about loving him and leaving him were about as clear as mud at the moment. How could she let him do this to her? How could one brief look at him set her hormones surging?

Well, she had it all figured out. Maybe.

When she turned, he still stood at the door staring at her, the late morning sunlight behind him, a peculiar expression on his face. He was a Nordic god, she reminded herself. She could just imagine him, his hair long and flowing in the breeze against his bronzed chest, standing at the stern of a Viking ship and peering out over the ocean. She inhaled deeply and sighed. She'd been reading too much lately, way too much.

But the way his shorts slung low on his hips heightened every sensitive nerve ending in her body. Her gaze played over the planes of his chest. His smattering of light brown chest hair glistened with a little morning perspiration, his glasses sat halfway down his nose, his hair was tousled, and he hadn't shaved in three days now.

He looked, well, good enough to eat.

"Where have you been?"

Tasha shook herself and realized she'd been musing for way too long. Andrew had closed the door, crossed the room, and was sitting in the rattan chair watching her.

"I got groceries."

Andrew scratched his head. "Groceries? Why? We can eat in the dining hall."

Tasha realized she was going to have to say something about yesterday. "Andrew, I . . . I just needed some time to hash things out in my mind."

"And did you?"

"Sort of. I got up early, did some meditating with Samuel."

"What did you decide?"

"I decided that . . . that we need to get away from here for a while."

"Away from the hotel?"

"Yes. How about a picnic?" she asked, risking a smile. "I don't know about you, but I'm about ready for a change of scenery. I've got some sandwich stuff and some fruit and I thought we'd check out the lake."

"Whoa." Andrew rose. "You went out this morning?"

"Oh, no. Josh helped me raid the kitchen fridge."

"If it will get me out of this hot room for a while, I'm game for just about anything. I'm about to climb the walls here. It was so hot last night I could barely sleep." He watched her face for a minute and Tasha had to wonder if that was the only reason he couldn't sleep.

"Yeah, well, I didn't sleep much either."

Andrew frowned. "You're the one who walked out of here yesterday, not me," he bluntly returned, his glare saying more than his words.

Tasha immediately wished she could take back her statement, but it was too late now. "So I'm the idiot, okay? I apologized. You can stop throwing darts at me."

"The least you could have done was tell me where you were."

So he had worried about her.

"I wasn't sure what I was going to do. I really didn't think you'd care." Tasha picked up the bags of groceries and headed for the door.

"I did care. Do care."

"I just walked for a while, okay? I took a long walk on the beach. Not the nude beach, the regular beach. I wanted to be by myself and think, okay?"

"Okay. Then let's go," he grumbled and met her at the door.

The walk to the lake took longer than Tasha expected, even though they followed the map exactly. That was just fine with Tasha. The more secluded, the better. She was looking forward to a peaceful afternoon. Maybe they could finally settle down a bit and learn a little more about each other, maybe even relax and spend an afternoon in pleasant conversation, not jumping down each other's throats.

The lake was small. An average-size wooden dock ran about midway out. A small aluminum boat, complete with oars, was tied to the dock. There was a sandy beach in front of them and a waterfall spilling into the lake behind them. They set up their picnic site on the edge of the sand under the shade of a huge palm. Trees and overgrown vegetation and tall grasses surrounded the rarely used lake, keeping it well hidden from view.

Such a peaceful, picture-perfect, secluded scene. Tasha couldn't have asked for anything better, and she felt kind of giddy.

She spread the picnic out on a blanket from her bed. She had brought a ham, cheese, lettuce, and tomato sandwich for Andrew, along with potato chips and several pints of milk. She'd also picked up some brownies for him for dessert—a conservative meal for a conservative kind of guy.

For herself—and him, if he wished—she'd bought a large hunk of cheddar cheese, some green grapes which left a lot to be desired but nevertheless were grapes, a bag of apples, and some carrots. She'd also found a can of mixed nuts, although she hated the amount of salt they contained, and some wanna-be granola bars. To drink, she was pleased to find bottled spring water. It wasn't like home, but it was close enough.

As she lifted the items out of the brown paper sacks and set them on the blanket, she chatted happily about what she'd brought for each of them. She glanced at Andrew, who sat and eyed her with curiosity. When she was finished and everything was in place to suit her, she sat back on her heels, satisfied. Then she turned her face up at him and smiled. "There," she sighed. "I think we're all ready now. Hungry?"

Andrew lifted a thick blond eyebrow, then sank down to lean on one elbow. He grinned back at her. "Amazing. I never would have dreamed."

"What?" Tasha asked, still smiling and pleased with herself.

"You. I wouldn't have thought there was a domestic bone in your body. I wouldn't have thought you got into this kind of stuff."

"What do you mean, *this kind of stuff?*" she asked in a stilted voice.

"You know," he continued. "Serving people."

Her smile faded. She sat perfectly still for a moment. "What do you mean by that?" she asked bluntly. The entire conversation had struck a bad chord with her and she needed clarification.

He chuckled—almost cautiously, Tasha thought, as if he were anticipating what was coming. "I just meant that I never had a mental picture of you serving anyone, that's all—getting all this stuff and laying it all out here so nice for me. Choosing the kind of food you thought I'd like— well, it all seems rather . . . domestic, what a dutiful little woman ought to do."

Dutiful—little—woman? For about twenty seconds, Tasha just sat there and looked at him, dumbfounded. Then, after she'd regained her senses, she sat up on her knees, picked up each article of food, and methodically put it all back into the bags. Her chest hurt from her pent-up anger, anger she wouldn't dare let out. If she did, she would explode.

How dare he ruin this!

Andrew watched her. She could feel it, but she wouldn't look him in the face. When she reached out to grab the ham and cheese sandwich, he placed his hand around her wrist. She tried to tug it away; he grasped tighter.

"Tasha . . ." he murmured softly.

"Let go of me," she spat at him, still staring at the ham and cheese sandwich.

With his other hand, Andrew reached over to cup her face and turn it to him. She resisted, but finally she let him pull her face close to his so she was looking him square in the jaw. His mouth and lips were entirely too close. She broke free, sat back on her haunches, placed her hands firmly on her hips, and met his gaze head on.

"All right, lay it all out on the line. Tell me what I said wrong this time. Let's get it over with," he ordered.

Tasha didn't know where to start, how to even say it so it would make sense to a man who might be from the Ice Age as far as his view were concerned. He didn't even understand what he had said that had her so riled.

"Okay! All right! You want to know what's the matter with me? Well, I'll tell you. I'm tired of your thinking I'm some feminist lunatic with a wacky lifestyle and no morals."

Surprised, Andrew interrupted, "I never said that, Tasha . . ."

She blinked. "Sure you have. You say it all the time."

"No, you're wrong. I've never said that."

"But you imply it."

"When? And what does this have to do with what I said a minute ago?"

Tasha was confused. Suddenly her head started throbbing. What *did* that have to do with what he'd said earlier? She wasn't sure. Where had that come from?

"It's . . . it's that domesticity thing you were throwing around. Damn it!" Tasha stood up, totally confused now as to what she really wanted to say. Then the tears started. "If I want to do something nice for you like pick out a damned ham and cheese sandwich because I think you might like it, then I'll do it simply because I want to do it! Not because I have any ulterior motives or feel some womanly urge to do so or want to get you out of your damned clothes! I simply wanted to!

"No," she continued angrily. "I'm not into subservience any more than the next woman, but, damn it, if I want to do something for a man, you or any man, I'll do it no matter what anyone says or thinks, any feminist, my mother—I don't give a damn what any one of them would think! I do what I want, when I want, and if that includes choosing to serve a man or any one else, for that matter, then so be it! I'm tired of this crap!" Looking down at her shaking hands through her blurred eyes, she realized she still held the ham sandwich. It was mangled in her hands.

"So here's your stupid ham sandwich, you creep! *Bon appétit!*"

It bounced off his chest with a thud and hit the blanket as Andrew stood unmoving before her.

ELEVEN

The forest around them fell silent after Tasha finished her tirade. She stood there, her gaze locked with his, tears still rolling down her cheeks. After a moment, Andrew stepped closer, avoiding the already ruined sandwich.

"I never said you had no morals," he whispered.

Tasha closed her eyes briefly then opened them again, wishing for once she'd kept it all inside. "I know." She slipped the fingers of both hands deep inside her denim shorts pockets and glanced past his shoulder.

"Then why did you say that?"

Taking in a ragged breath, Tasha brought her gaze back to his face. His eyes looked full of hurt. She suspected hers did, too. She shrugged her shoulders. "Who knows? My insecurities are showing, I guess. I really don't know what you think of me. You know, because I . . . I teased you the other day at the beach . . . about . . . about the volleyball game."

Andrew stepped closer. With a forefinger, he smoothed her tears off each cheek. Tasha closed her eyes, feeling she might melt at his touch. "I don't think any less of you," he replied quietly. "In fact, it makes me think more highly of you."

"Why?" She wouldn't look at him.

"Because you stick to your convictions and don't back down for anything or anyone."

Eyes still closed, Tasha trembled and felt his hands grasp her upper arms to pull her closer. "I do think you're crazy sometimes." He chuckled quietly for just a second.

Tasha no sooner opened her eyes then she closed them again, for in about the same instant, Andrew's lips gently found hers, pressing, nibbling, and sending quivers down her already trembling spine. Then he released her.

Tasha looked at Andrew, wondering how all this had transpired so quickly. Caught unaware by his kiss, she didn't quite know what to do or to say.

"I'm sorry. I didn't mean anything earlier. And . . . I'm sorry about yesterday. I shouldn't have thrown such a fit."

She nodded. "I shouldn't have thrown such a fit today."

"We're even then?"

She nodded, watching his face.

"Your point was well taken, though."

"Was it?" she asked, wide-eyed.

Andrew gathered her close and held her to him, laying her head on his shoulder, threading his fingers through the strands of her hair. "Yes. We're so different, I just don't know what to do about it."

Tasha nodded against him. "I know," she whispered softly. Deep inside, though, she knew what had to be done. And she'd already made that very clear to him.

An hour later they were finishing up the remnants of their picnic, still picking over what was left of the bunch of grapes, trying to find any salvageable enough to eat.

"Do you eat like this all the time?" Andrew asked, sitting with his knees propped up in front of him, his back against the tree.

Tasha, lying on her side at the edge of the blanket, her head resting on her hand, finished chewing the last grape she'd popped into her mouth before answering. "Like what?"

"Fresh stuff. Fruits and vegetables. Are you a health nut?"

She shrugged. "Not really. I do eat lots of fruits and vegetables, though, especially the ones I sell in my shop."

"That's right, you said you sold vegetables."

"Organically grown fruits and vegetables and vitamins and herbal remedies. I'm a part-time herbalist and all-around health expert, you might say, although I have to admit I don't practice what I preach all the time. Dairy products are my weakness. What about you?"

"Red meat and potatoes. Hasn't hurt me yet." He pounded his chest in a macho-man way.

Tasha ignored him. "Probably with mushy green beans smothered in pork fat on the side," she added sarcastically.

"Umm. And cornbread."

"Of course," Tasha returned and rolled her eyes. "With lots of butter, I'm sure."

"Didn't I tell you we were originally from the south? My mother still cooks like that—fried chicken, grits, gravy, bacon drippings in everything."

Tasha grimaced. "I didn't know anyone still cooked like that. Look, you have to agree nice, crisp steamed green beans are so much better for you. You retain all the nutrients and the flavor that way. The way you eat them, they're not doing diddly for your body nutritionally and it just adds all those fat grams."

Andrew stretched his arms over his head then lazily stretched out next to her. His face held the most unusual smirk, she thought as he leaned closer. He was no more than a foot away, and Tasha wasn't quite sure what was coming next. "I dare you to find one stray ounce of fat on my body."

Tasha felt her eyes widen. He was right. There wasn't an ounce of fat anywhere on that body. But she liked a challenge. "Take off your shirt."

In one swift movement, he did. How had that happened so easily? Tasha asked herself. She'd been trying to get him out of that shirt for days now. Her eyes dropped to his chest, lean and firm all the way to his waist. His dark blond chest hair tapered to a darker point just at his belt.

"So." Tasha breathed deeply and looked at his face. "You work out much?" she asked.

"I lift weights some. Play a little handball."

"Oh, well," she continued, glancing past his

CRAZY FOR YOU 163

body toward the cool lake. *It sure is getting hot out here.* "Then you're burning it all off, but that doesn't mean you're healthy."

His eyes locked with hers. "I'm healthy, believe me. Fit as a fiddle and lots of stamina."

"Oh." *I'll bet.* Tasha glanced away.

He picked up a tendril of her hair and began twirling it between his fingers. Tasha knew it was impossible, but it felt as if her hair had nerve endings all its own that took pleasure in his caress. A slow fire began eating away within her. It was damned hot out here.

"Yeah, and I owe it all to my mother's down-home country cooking."

Tasha cocked her head sideways at him. Her hair slid out of his fingers. "You don't still live with your mother, do you?" she asked bluntly.

Andrew reached for a carrot and bit off a chunk. Chewing slowly—and if a person could chew seductively, he was—Tasha watched as he rolled the vegetable between his fingertips and contemplated her. "What if I do?"

"I'd say you were too old to be a mama's boy," she returned quickly. "Either that or you were an only child or a spoiled brat and you still want the pampering."

Andrew chuckled. "False on all accounts. No, I don't still live at home. It would, believe it or not"—he lowered his brow at her—"cramp my lifestyle a bit. And I was far from a spoiled brat or the only child. I was the middle child who always got left out and who turned out to be the pleaser to get attention. I think that's why I'm such a workaholic. I had to work a little harder than the rest to get anyone's attention when I was growing up."

Tasha thought about all that for a second. "Bet you had the whole nine yards growing up, didn't you? The kids, the stay-at-home mom, the dad who brought home the bacon, church on Sundays, the dog, and the picket fence."

Andrew nodded hesitantly, a strange look on his face. "Well, yes. What about you?"

What about *me?* Tasha rolled over onto her back, threaded her fingers together across her abdomen, and stared up at the turquoise sky. She sighed deeply. Different worlds.

"My life growing up was so far removed from that little scenario you probably couldn't fathom it." Trepidation crept over her for a moment, but she pushed it aside.

"Try me."

It was the way he grinned at her just then, when she looked up at him, that made her go on. It was one of those come-hither grins, the kind that curled a man's lip up at the corner and curled a woman's toes in the process. A thin-lipped Kevin Costner grin—the kind that said I'm a little bit amazed at you and I don't know quite what to do with you yet. She liked that grin, she decided, even it was confusing the hell out of her. She tried not to think about it.

"In a nutshell, my parents were and still are hippies, definite throwbacks. I'm an only child, conceived in the late sixties during a kind of Woodstock-type music event out in Colorado. I grew up in a small mountain town where, for a while, we lived in a commune with several other families during the early seventies. The adults grew the food and sold flowers and probably some other things that were somewhat illegal. I was too young to really remember much. We kids had our chores, but we played in the fields more than we worked.

"My mother's name is Violet Rainbow. She's into holistic medicine and crystals—you know, all the New Age stuff. My father's name is Zeus, and he repairs mountain bikes. Of course, those aren't their real names.

"My full real name is Moontasha Begonia. As my parents once said, Smith was such a plain name they wanted us to stand out in the world. We've all been on a perpetual Rocky Mountain high—a natural one, that is—for as long as I can remember, valuing nature and her gifts and trying to avoid commercialism, yuppieism, and the all-American dream.

"To put it bluntly, I grew up eating alfalfa sprouts and tofu and wouldn't know a picket fence if I saw one. I guess you and I are about as far apart in backgrounds as two people could be." For a fleeting moment, it bothered the hell out of her, just as it had in high school when she'd tried to be something she wasn't.

Andrew had rolled over onto his stomach and looked down at her as she spoke. His eyes had narrowed, and he was chewing on his inner lip. She'd blown it now, she could tell. She'd just confirmed every crazy thought he'd had about her.

"You made all that up, didn't you?"

The corner of Tasha's mouth drew up and she shook her head slightly as she chuckled. "All the truth, I swear it." Well, at least it was all out on the line. She never had been one to pull punches.

"You are one hell of an interesting woman, Moontasha Begonia Smith."

"Yeah." She reached up and chucked his chin with her fist lightly. "And you're about as foreign to me as an alien. But I'm willing to put that all aside if you are." The second the statement was out of her mouth, Tasha panicked. Why had she said that?

His eyes searched her face for a brief moment. "Consider it shoved way out of the way."

She nodded her agreement. "It's done." Her gaze caught his and held it for a long moment. *Okay. So what does this all mean?*

Andrew lowered his head and gently brushed his lips across hers for the second time that day. The tingles that brief kiss generated stayed with her long after he'd rolled over onto his side, his arm bent to support his head, to look at her.

"So what about all this herbal stuff you sell in your store? Isn't that mostly a hoax? Are you the snake oil salesman?" He reached over to pull another strand of hair toward him. He brought it to his nose and sniffed. "You smell good, by the way."

Tasha swallowed a huge dry lump in her throat. For three days now, she had been pursuing him and he had done just about everything to put her off. Now the tables were turning. He was sending signals—*those* signals. Good vibes were strumming around them. Then why did everything seem a little off center all of a sudden?

Why was she breathing from deep in her chest?

"Uh . . . herbal remedies. Well, no, they're not a hoax. It's really very scientific, if you do your research. Herbs have been around as long as man and man has been using them for all kinds of medicinal and health purposes for millennia."

"For example?" He rubbed her hair across his lips. Tasha's libido leaped.

"For example . . . ah, well, a very good example would be . . . for . . . contraception."

"Contraception." He repeated the word as he dropped her hair. His eyes widened.

"Uh-huh," Tasha squeaked, flipping her hair back over her shoulder. "For instance"—her gaze scanned the land around them as she leaned up on one elbow—"Queen Anne's lace."

"Queen Anne's lace will prevent pregnancy?" He eyed her suspiciously.

"So they tell me. I've never used it myself, but I've studied herbs a bit. From what I've learned, a teaspoon full of Queen Anne's lace seeds taken with a glass of water immediately after sex will prevent pregnancy. I don't advertise that. The government would probably come after me if I did. But some women in rural areas even today use the seeds to prevent pregnancies."

"You mean in foreign countries?"

"I mean in Virginia, North Carolina, Tennessee. Appalachia."

"You're kidding."

"I kid you not."

"Amazing. So what else?"

Tasha shrugged. "Well, nutritionally, there's all kinds of things. Peppermint tea is good for headaches and to calm a jumpy stomach, chamomile is good for the nervous system and menstrual cramps, yarrow is great for flu and fevers, and sarsaparilla's a good diuretic." She paused for a second before she went on. He seemed to be listening intently.

"Bee pollen is wonderful for strength and endurance," she continued, "and if your dog has fleas, an extract made of pennyroyal mixed with water as a spray seems to work miracles and is less harmful to the animal. Ginseng is good for all kinds of things like blood pressure, the immune system, and stress, not to mention it's a mild sexual stimulant. But many herbs make that claim—damiana, for one, shou wu sho for another. Plus there are other combinations that are supposed to work wonderfully."

She'd been picking at the bunch of grapes in front of her as she spoke, and now, as the breeze lifted her hair and a small insect buzzed, it was all but silent around them. Contraceptives and sexual stimulants? Couldn't she pick other topics to talk about?

Tasha looked up at him.

"But I wouldn't know about those, of course. I've never tried them."

"Uh . . . huh." He uttered the two syllables very slowly and leaned forward. "Tell me more."

Her lips were dry, really dry, and Tasha scraped

her tongue over her lips to moisten them. His eyes followed the trail of her tongue. Then his lips parted slightly and she felt his warm breath against her cheek—they were that close. She was trembling inside.

"It's hot."

"Umm-hmmm," he inched closer. "You can say that again," he whispered. His lips were barely centimeters away from hers and Tasha's heart was beating wildly. His eyes were bedroomy as he drew closer. She didn't know if she could stand it any longer. This wasn't in the plan.

She snapped her fingers loudly and jerked her head back. "I've got a great idea. Let's swim!"

Tasha jumped to her feet, hesitated only a fraction of a second, then jogged off down the beach. As she did, she peeled off her T-shirt and tossed it aside, then kicked off her low-cut canvas sneakers. Her faded denim cutoffs came next. She wiggled out of them, hopping first on one foot, then the other. Last, but certainly not least, she slid out of her skimpy panties and kicked them backward toward Andrew. All the while, she ordered her pulse to kick into low gear and her brain to stop sending signals to her hormones. She was ready to explode.

She splashed into thigh-high water and dived in.

TWELVE

Andrew stood.

As he watched her run down to the lake, peeling off her clothing as she did, his libido surged into action. How in the world had this woman wormed her way into his life and his heart so quickly? And she *was* in his heart. He was a goner. Never had he felt such a physical reaction to a woman.

Andrew lifted his glasses off his face and gently laid them on the blanket. He took a step forward, then another. With each one, he hurried a little more, his body taking over, forcing him into longer strides to get closer to her.

His fingers fumbled with the laces of his shoes as he stumbled down the beach, tripping once, twice. He tossed his shoes over his shoulders. His purple socks followed. As his hands lifted to his waist and he wrestled with his zipper of his shorts, a torrent of desire deep within him urged his clumsy, shaking fingers on. With jerking movements, he lowered the zipper, hastily stepped out of the shorts, and left them in a heap at the water's edge.

All the while, he watched the back of Tasha's

head as she bobbed in the water halfway out to the dock. Every once in a while, she would dive under, allowing him a glimpse of her fully rounded little rear. Within seconds, he hit the water with a splash, diving into the cool depths.

Underneath, he swam until his lungs nearly burst. The soft, cool water caressed his naked body, but did nothing to put out the fire raging within him.

For that he was thankful. He had a better idea of how to put out that fire.

With aching muscles and bursting lungs, he broke the surface not far from Tasha with a churning of water. She turned as she treaded water and looked at him, her eyes wide, a questioning expression on her face. Her long hair, silky and shiny from the water, was slicked away from her forehead and floated about her shoulders. Her lips parted, and he urged himself closer to her.

As he floated nearer, he reached out to touch her cheek. She kicked away from him, the same expression on her face. Then suddenly smiled—a wicked smile—and Andrew's passion soared. He wanted her, damn it, and he wanted her now. He'd bet his last client she wanted him just as much.

Kicking to propel himself closer, he smiled back, only to get a face full of water splashed off Tasha's feet.

Okay, so that's the way we're going to play it?

She disappeared under the water. For what seemed a small eternity, the water became calm and quiet about him. He treaded water slowly, glancing about for something, anything, to indicate where she was . . . that she was all right. That she was coming back to him.

"Tasha," he whispered, but only the breeze heard him. He turned fully in the water, his eyes frantically searching. "Tasha . . . ?"

Then he felt her. Softly, gently, her hands found his thighs, his waist, his chest. As if in slow motion, she arched her body like a mermaid's and pushed herself up toward the surface of the water, sliding, caressing against him all the way. Andrew tossed his head back and squeezed his eyes shut in ecstasy at the desire that rippled through his body. Then he clasped his arms around her after she broke the surface, letting his palms glide over the smooth skin of her back.

Slowly, he dragged his gaze down to her face, searching her soulful eyes rimmed with water-spiked lashes. His hands framed her face, pulling her closer. Her hands rested on his shoulders. Her breasts flattened against his chest, urging him to pull her closer, closer until his fingers slid down her arms to grasp her waist, tugging her body into his.

Tasha's legs raked against his thighs as she treaded water beneath them. As their bodies met fully, as if by instinct, she grasped his shoulders tighter and wrapped her legs around his waist, shifting him even closer into the cradle of her thighs.

Unable to stand the closeness of their bodies any longer without releasing some of his pent-up passion, Andrew captured a fistful of her hair with one hand and with the other held her back. His lips descended on hers, and she took them, crushing, biting, bruising, neither stopping for a breath of air. They took of each other as if it were their last dying breath, their last chance at passion. Tasha's fingers kneaded his shoulders and his neck, pushing him into her. His tongue penetrated her mouth, drawing out the sweet, unbridled, honeyed passion he'd searched for all his life, but had never known.

Yes, he had never known this.

Then his legs, weak from treading water to keep them both afloat and from the passion that had totally overtaken his body, gave out. Soundlessly, their shoulders, their necks, their faces slipped beneath the surface of the lake, lips mingling, hands searching, until their lungs could stand no more. Breaking free of each other, they propelled their bodies toward the surface, Tasha breaking the water's calm first, Andrew following. As Tasha swam for the dock, Andrew followed automatically, his arms churning the water to get to her. His brain reeled with the thought that the simple absence of her body against his was the most painful thing he'd ever experienced.

Tasha tried once to hoist herself up on the deck, but the muscles in her biceps and shoulders had turned to jelly, so she slipped back down into the water. Again, she reached for the wooden dock, tensed her muscles, and pulled with all her energy. This time, she succeeded. With Andrew closing in on her fast, she rose out of the water and stepped across the warm dock. Water sluiced from her nude body, making intricate patterns across the weathered wood. Finding a smooth spot, she lay down on the wood, careful to avoid splinters, tossed back her hair, and propped herself up with her two elbows.

Smiling, she turned toward Andrew as, in one swift motion, he hoisted himself onto the dock. In a few strides, he was at her side, also dripping—and magnificent. Looking up at him, all her convictions were confirmed. He was a delicious, breathtaking hunk of human male, with water glistening like oil off his wide, only slightly tanned chest, his blue eyes penetrating her gaze as she perused his body, his narrow hips and waist, his thighs that didn't quit, and . . . oh my, yes, he was definitely all male. She gasped and her eyes widened in anticipation continuing what they had started in the lake.

Andrew raked his gaze over her, then silently slipped down to the dock beside her.

They were alone.
Andrew liked the idea of not sharing Tasha with the others. Thank God she'd found this place and convinced him to come with her.

Tasha turned her face up to him. The words that slipped off her tongue threw him for only a second. "Ever been in love, Andrew? I mean really in love?"

For a moment, he let the question linger in the air. Were her feelings that strong? Did they go beyond the simple desire to possess his body for an afternoon or a couple of days? Was it love?

Idle chatter, he told himself. With Tasha, he could always expect the opposite of the norm. But what if . . . what if she did want to speak of love? Of *their* love—if that, indeed, existed?

He decided to be straightforward with her. No matter what the reasoning behind her question, he owed her the truth.

"Yes, a while back I was in love with someone." He met her stare head on.

She adjusted her lithe body on her right side to face him. "Tell me."

Swallowing the dry lump in his throat, Andrew contemplated her curiosity. The passion between them moments earlier was waning, but he had no doubt it would take only seconds for it to explode again. Suddenly, it seemed important that they talk, that they discuss the past. It might even be important for their future.

"I was engaged once, three years ago. And, yes, I was in love with her."

"Was she your first?"

Andrew felt the right corner of his mouth draw up in a grin. "My first what?" he teased.

Tasha slanted her body closer to him. "Lover," she whispered in a low, devil-may-care voice.

He leaned in even closer, his lips barely centimeters from hers. Her eyes fluttered as he peered into them. "Maybe . . . maybe not."

Tasha slowly retreated. Dragging her left hand

up from her side, she combed all five fingers through her damp hair and flipped it out and over the plank decking in a nonchalant manner. Slowly, she turned her gaze back to him.

"But you didn't get married." It was a statement, not a question.

Andrew shook his head and looked at the short expanse of wood between them. Reaching out, he traced the weathered grain in the plank with his forefinger, the backs of his knuckles grazing her abdomen, then shifted his body to look her more fully in the face. "No," he said quietly. "She died two weeks before the wedding."

Tasha's eyes grew wide and dark with concern and compassion. She reached out and touched his forearm. "I'm sorry. I shouldn't have asked."

"No." He shook his head and looked again at the dock. "It's all right. I'm okay. It was tough at the time, but I'm okay." When he brought his gaze back to her face, she saw it was true. He was okay.

"Tell me about her." The teasing quality in her voice was gone.

Andrew angled a glance her way. "Why?"

Shrugging her left shoulder, a shy grin played across her face. "I'd like to know about her, unless it makes you uncomfortable."

"No," he interrupted. "It doesn't make me uncomfortable."

"Okay."

Shifting to a more comfortable position, Andrew settled in for the long haul. If he could, he'd make it as short and sweet as possible. It had been three years, but the pain was still there. However minute, it was still there.

"Diana was petite and blond with blue eyes."

"Just like you. I mean the blond and blue eyes part," she chuckled.

Smiling, Andrew nodded. "Yes, I guess so. She was a teacher, elementary school. Grew up in Seattle. In fact, I knew her most of my life."

"High-school sweethearts?" Tasha interjected. When he looked at her, he knew she already knew the answer.

"Yes, but we went to separate universities, started our careers, and then decided to get married."

Tasha snorted. "Just like good little yuppies should." She regretted the statement as soon as it was out of her mouth. "Sorry, that was uncalled for."

Andrew was unsure what that last remark meant. "We did what we thought was right. Sometimes I wish we'd eloped right after high school. At least that way we would have had some time together. As it stands, we never had a chance."

Tasha stared over Andrew's left shoulder. Off in the distance, cotton-candy clouds floated in the breeze. A perfect day, she thought. Such a tragedy he had suffered. It couldn't have happened on a day like this, could it? Could this beautiful world bring about a tragedy such as that?

"How did she die?" She averted her eyes.

"At the hands of a seventeen-year-old kid who thought he could do seventy in a residential area and forget about four-way stops. It snuffed out both their lives. I was devastated. So was my family and hers. The kid's folks . . . they were pitiful. He was their only child. It was insane."

"Andrew," Tasha reached out again and touched his arm. "I'm so sorry."

He ignored her touch and stared off into the blue sky. Right now, the emotions within him thrashed back and forth from the pain of remembrance to the reality of his desire for Tasha, confusing emotions that raced out of control. He focused on the only thing he could grasp at the moment, his memories. For some reason, he needed to play the scenario all the way through.

"She was so much like me," he whispered. "She was perfect for me. We'd planned everything—the house we would build, how many kids we would have, their names, everything. And it was all taken away so damned quickly." He closed his eyes at the pain.

"You had planned children?"

Turning back to her, his eyes met hers and held. Children . . . how would Tasha be with children? He chuckled inwardly, the only way he could erase the pain. He could just picture her children in his mind—long-haired, thin and tan and healthy, eating raw carrots and granola for snacks, learning how to be environmentally safe while trying to save the ozone, all the while strumming their guitars and humming "Kum Bah Yah." And Tasha would be right beside them, loving every minute of it.

She would be a wonderful mother.

"Yes." His eyes still held fast to hers. "We

thought a lot about children. Of course, Diana always said she would stay home with them during the early years, then go back to teaching."

"Of course," Tasha whispered. "That's important."

"And she'd read to them and prepare them for school."

"I can imagine." Tasha stared off again, over his shoulder. Andrew would have given a hundred-dollar bill for her thoughts.

"And run them to ballet and music lessons and ball practice," he continued.

". . . and feed the dog and bake cookies and paint the picket fence, too," she barely murmured.

Andrew reached out to touch her chin, bringing her gaze back even with his as he took in the strained quality of her voice.

"Yes," she said as she looked into his eyes. It was as if she was trying not to tremble at his touch, trying not to show that the thought of his and Diana's mythical children disturbed her. He could tell it had. "I'll bet she was perfect for you."

"She was." He dipped his head into a questioning half nod, his finger still lingering on her chin.

"Not like me," Tasha supplied halfheartedly.

"Diana was nothing like you."

"Oh," she lowered her gaze to the space between them.

But I don't want you to be, he wanted to say to her, but didn't. *I don't want you to be Diana.* The words wouldn't come. Not yet. "Somehow I can't see you whitewashing the picket fence."

Tasha tensed. "No, probably not. Nary a picket fence in my future." *The thing is,* she told herself, *someday I might actually want that picket fence more than I realize.*

But she'd never tell him that. Fingers of panic skittered across her abdomen. Suddenly it seemed all important that she did tell him.

She looked at him. "So you don't think I'm the picket-fence type?"

Andrew smiled a crooked smile and Tasha wasn't sure he knew how to respond. "I-I'm not sure."

She didn't want to hear any more about picket fences or former lovers. She didn't want to think any more about what she did or didn't want Andrew to know about her. This was getting complicated. And she didn't quite know why, but it made her damned uncomfortable to believe Andrew thought she wouldn't fit in the picket-fence world.

Well, he was probably right. There was no use fighting it.

Abruptly, Tasha rolled over onto her back, breaking free of his touch on her chin. Feigning indifference to the whole previous conversation, she lay there for a few moments, breathing evenly and deeply, hoping to convince Andrew she'd gone to sleep.

Hoping to communicate to him she wished she'd never asked him about being in love.

Watching her, Andrew immediately noticed the change in the atmosphere around them. Her facial features, at first tight and tense, slowly relaxed as she breathed evenly in and out. Finally, it seemed she'd wrestled whatever demon lay within her and had reached a conclusion. He wished he could do the same.

The notion that Diana was so much like himself bothered her. He knew why. Why he didn't tell her he understood, he didn't know. She was frightened to think their differences—his and Tasha's—would keep them apart. The more he thought about it, the more he knew how much of a kink that could throw into their relationship. With Diana, he had known exactly how his life would be laid out. With Tasha, he'd be lucky to predict what would occur within minutes. Daisies and onions. It would never work, and she knew it. So did he.

"What about you?" Andrew watched her eyelids flutter open.

"What about me?"

"Have you ever been truly in love?"

Her eyes closed. "No," she whispered.

The afternoon held the silence like a saturated sponge. Andrew watched her face. It tensed, then, after a while, relaxed. There was something more she wasn't telling him. He waited.

"There's a man back home in Colorado. His name is Mark Tyler. I left him standing at the altar a little over a month ago." She sat up then and turned toward him, propping her head on her bent elbow. "But I'm sure you don't want to hear about that."

"I want to hear anything you want to tell me."

Andrew watched her face, realizing how important it was she share this with him.

She lowered her gaze to the deck. "Mark and I grew up together. We've been really great friends, best friends, I guess you could say, since first grade. He's always been there for me. He always was there. About a year ago, he started telling me he loved me and wanted to marry me. At first I resisted. Then I thought, why not?" She looked into Andrew's eyes.

"I love Mark, but it's not the type of love I should have for a husband. I knew that, but I agreed to marry him. I wanted to make him happy. I thought I would be happy. Finally, I realized all I was doing was making us miserable. I'd pretty much done that all our lives together. He'd always loved me. I'd always broken his heart. Somehow, he always came back for more."

Tasha shifted against the deck and heaved a big sigh. Andrew watched her gaze drift off over his shoulder. He simply waited and listened.

"He's such a good man. I don't deserve his friendship."

"Don't say that."

Her gaze shifted to meet his eyes. "I'm a pretty all-around rotten person. Haven't you realized that yet? I'm beginning to think the only place I belong is in the apartment above my shop in that little rinky-dink mountain town where everybody understands me. Except Mark, of course. Right about now he doesn't understand me at all."

Andrew reached out and touched her shoulder. "Why do you beat yourself up so? There's nothing wrong with you, Tasha," he returned softly. "You've never been in love. So what? I think you were right for not going ahead with your marriage to Mark. You both would have been miserable. You've learned from your mistakes and you've grown from them."

"Have I? I'm not sure if I've grown at all from this thing with Mark—or from life, for that matter. In fact, I haven't spoken to him since the day I called off our plans. I've been acting like a spoiled little girl. When I was moping around in a blue funk for a month at my shop, that's when my mother gave me this trip to get me out of the house and make me stop wallowing in my misfortune. I thought I could get my head together to go back and face him. But now"—she let her gaze play over his face—"now I'm more confused than ever."

"About loving him?"

Tasha quickly shook her head. "No. Not that. I've always known I didn't love him the way I should in order to marry him. I know I have to talk to him when I get back. I'm just confused about . . . other things. Feelings."

Andrew held her gaze for another brief moment. He touched his fingertips to the back of her cheek. "I know," he whispered. "I feel that way myself."

THIRTEEN

"Isn't this wonderful?" Tasha asked Andrew. He glanced at her as she leaned back on the dock looking up into the sky. They had sat in silence for the past several minutes.

It was as if she'd come to terms with what was at hand and was willing to leave it alone. He was glad they'd cleared the obstacles of their pasts. All that remained were the obstacles of the future. Those might not be quite as easy to break down. Tasha knew what she needed to do concerning Mark, that was apparent, and they both knew they needed to come to terms with what was happening between them.

"What?" His glance at her willed her to look at him. She did.

"This . . . finally we're free." Eyes closed, she tossed her head back, her hair cascading down her back to the dock. She arched her neck as if paying homage to the sun. "We've shed the trappings of our society, Andrew. We're at one with nature. We don't need our clothing. All we need is our bodies, ourselves. It's just as Samuel said it would be."

Andrew tipped his head closer to her, taking in

the relaxed expression on her face. He liked it better. The old Tasha was back, and his libido was churning into action as his gaze played over the smooth arch of her neck. "Yes," he supplied seductively. "I wholeheartedly agree. . . ."

Tasha's eyes shot open. Taking in the expression in her eyes, he watched as she stretched her arms over her head and lay fully across the deck. She lazily closed her eyes again. Her breasts thrust upward into the increasingly warm afternoon sunshine. She lifted one knee slightly off the dock as she continued to stretch and arch her body like a cat. Andrew's eyes were drawn down the length of her body from the tips of her fingernails to her toes, momentarily lingering on each significant and luxurious body part in between. If she opened her eyes, she would know exactly what was on his mind.

"The orientation session was right, you know." Tasha spoke again from her languid position beside him, her face still tilted toward the sky. "I've never in my life felt so relaxed, so uninhibited, so full of a sense of self. So terribly free. I never dreamed by removing my clothing and baring my bodily imperfections I could feel so—"

Andrew had had just about all he could stand. Imperfections, hell! There wasn't one single flaw on that gorgeous, sensuous body! Didn't she know that? Didn't she realize she was driving him crazy?

Reaching over, he grasped her chin in his hand and dipped his head closer to hers. As he pulled her closer to him, her eyes flew open in surprise.

But before he would allow even a whimper, he crushed his lips down on hers.

"Don't . . . you . . . ever . . . shut . . . up?" he growled between nibbles and quick thrusts of his tongue against her lips.

"Sometimes," she answered breathlessly as she brought her hands up around his neck, pulling him closer.

Andrew leaned forward to partially cover her body with his. Her left leg slid up of his thigh and rested against his right side. Desire, deep and apparent to them both, coursed through him to her, heating their flesh every place their skin touched—which was just about everywhere. The gentle rolling of the dock rocked them into the cradles their bodies made for each other. Andrew moaned and dragged his right hand down from her chin to her neck, lingering on one breast to gently thumb the peaked nipple, then lower to the small curve of her belly. And again lower until he reached the place he sought—the hot and tender, moist and yielding center of her body. He cupped her. She moaned, her lips still connected with his. He penetrated her with a finger. She trembled, her breath hot against his cheek. He found what pleasured her and firmly grasped her there, molding the shape of her into his palm, kneading her with his fingertips. She arched into him, gasping his name between her frantic hot bursts of breath, her hands clutching his shoulders.

"Tasha . . ." he whispered into her hair. "Do

you realize how long I've needed to touch you like this?"

She nodded and moaned back her answer.

Forgetting everything, he flung one leg over her lower body, his hand still cupping and caressing his prized possession, his other arm pillowing her head to cradle her closer into him so he could capture her lips, her eyes, her cheeks and ears and neck with his mouth.

Ah, his sweet Tasha. . . .

Her fingernails dug into his shoulder as his ministrations below caused her lower body to tense.

"Let it go, honey," he whispered into her hair as he found the sweet spot behind her ear. "Let it go. Flow into me, baby. I want to make you feel more alive and free than you ever have in your life."

Tasha was wrong. Being nude wasn't the most freeing experience she'd ever had. Being nude and making love with Andrew, out in the open air with the baby blue sky above and Mother Nature all around, was the most exhilarating, intimate passionate oneness with nature she ever dared to experience.

She'd lost herself the moment he touched her, forgetting all her earlier fears. His fingers, his hands, his lips were everywhere, sending her into trembling, indescribable desire. Never before had she felt like this.

Never.

He whispered into her ear and she moaned

back incoherently. He stroked her, and the banked fire within her ignited, burning, scorching his palm, she knew. She was on fire, and he had done that to her. He had set her free, had ignited a passion so deep within her she'd forgotten it was ever there. Perhaps it never was there. As the fury grew, she clutched and clawed at him, lost in the moment and the flood of emotions and feelings, only wanting more, more of him.

In every way. . . .

Then she erupted against his hand, the flames licking high within her. His body arched into hers, holding her close. He held her and murmured in her ear, caressingly, slowly bringing her back to awareness.

Finally, Tasha stirred, burrowing closer against him. Andrew sighed, pulled her close, and smoothed the hair falling down her back.

Smiling, Tasha nuzzled his chest. "You told me the other day I was about to explode," she whispered. "I think I just did."

Andrew cupped her delicate face in his hands so he could see every expression on her face, thankful of the simple gift they had just shared, the closeness, the intimacy. There was no comparison. Ever. And he would never forget it.

Reaching up, she traced the outline of his cheekbone. "Now it's your turn," she breathed back at him.

Andrew groaned, then rolled over onto her fully.

Oh, God, how I want her.

A wild screech broke the quiet afternoon, startling them both. Andrew and Tasha shifted to see what was going on. Intermittent shrieks and yells added to the commotion. Every bird in the surrounding trees took flight at the intrusion.

" 'Ey, look, mon, tourists!"

Andrew and Tasha froze.

Startled, Tasha jumped to her feet. Andrew quickly followed, then stepped slightly in front of her, shielding her body from full view of the scene before them.

"Oh, hell," Tasha whispered behind Andrew's back. "There goes the neighborhood."

"Shhh," he ordered quietly. "Let me handle it. Do exactly as I say. I don't think they're going to come all the way after us or anything. I think we're safe out here. Just keep quiet."

"I hope you're right." She burrowed into his back, glad for once she could rely on someone to protect her.

With wild laughter, howls of delight, loud bursts of reggae music, and chortling motorbike engines, the kids ran over Tasha and Andrew's picnic lunch, the blanket, and their clothing—grinding them all into the sand.

Then they circled one last time and stopped, pointing the noses of their bikes toward Tasha and Andrew.

"Jump!" she called out. They dived into the water.

Tasha and Andrew gripped the ladder behind the dock, searching each other's faces. They had waited a few minutes, heard the bikes and the music fade away, and were hoping their visitors were gone.

"Do you think they've left?" she whispered.

Shrugging his shoulders, Andrew started up the ladder. "I'll look."

He was back down in a second. Tasha wasn't sure she liked the look on his face.

"Well?" she prompted.

"They're gone."

"So let's get out of here, okay? I keep getting this creepy sensation all up and down my spine." She started to ascend the ladder herself.

Andrew grabbed her arm. "Wait."

She turned to him, eyes wide. "What?"

"There's something I didn't tell you. They took some things."

"Things?"

"Our clothes."

She gave him a look of pure shock—eyes round, brows arched, lips clamped together in a firm, thin line. She wasted no more time climbing up and out of the water to the top of the deck.

Andrew followed. They stood looking out to the beach.

In another second, she ran to the edge of the dock and dived into the water.

Reaching out to pull handfuls of water toward and away from her, Tasha churned at the water until her feet reached the smooth, mossy bottom. Finally, she reached the sand, jogged up on the beach, and confirmed Andrew's words. When she

CRAZY FOR YOU 191

heard Andrew's labored breathing behind her, she turned to him.

"They took our clothes!"

Andrew's face grew frantic. "I know!" He glanced around the area before and behind them, searching, pacing back and forth across the hot sand. He looked into a garbage can a few feet away and then behind the big palm that had shaded them earlier. He was definitely agitated about the whole mess.

"They're gone, Andrew. Give it up."

"My glasses! I need my glasses!" Then he stepped on something. He leaned over to pick it up and then held it out in front of him.

"I think you found them." Tasha looked at the mangled wire. "Do you need them that much?"

After a moment, Andrew shook his head, then flung them aside. "I can live without them for a while," he grumbled.

He turned back to his search.

"Ah-hah!" Andrew waded into waist high grass behind the tree to retrieve something. "I've found something!" But when he pulled it out, it was the blanket, not their clothing.

"Come out of there, Andrew! You'll get bug bites—"

Up to your delicious little behind, you idiot.

"You'll be sor-ry," she sang out.

"I'm going to find our clothes, damn it," he called back to her as he thrashed through the grasses and weeds. "Don't you see what a predicament this is?"

Tasha walked to the edge of the sand. "I see

perfectly well what the predicament is. A, we've got to walk back to the resort. B, we've got no clothing to wear. C, we don't really know where those scoundrels are who took our clothing and if they're coming back. D, you're going to be scratching from here to kingdom come if you don't get your cute little behind out of those weeds. Oh, and E, your back is really red. I think you're getting a nasty sunburn."

He popped up out of the weeds. "All the more reason for you to get your fanny out here and help me," he glowered at her.

"Andrew . . ."

He turned to her again, his eyes desperate. "Don't you see? They took my clothes. My *clothes*. What am I going to do?"

Shaking her head, Tasha stared back at him. "We'll figure out something. We can go shopping when we get back."

"When we get back? What about getting from here to there? That's what I'm most concerned with." He looked up at her. "Look, are you gonna help me, or what?"

Tasha huffed and settled her hands on her hips, forgetting the tiny niggling voice, forgetting everything but their present predicament. "If you think I'm stepping one foot into those weeds, Andrew Powell, then you've got another think coming. I'm not particularly fond of chigger bites on my—"

"Yow!" Andrew jumped up like a shot. Within seconds, he was back at her side, thrusting his hand out to her. "Get it off!" he shouted. "Get if off, now!"

Tasha grasped his hand. "Hold still," she ordered, looking down at the bee still partially attached to its stinger, which was imbedded in the fleshy part of Andrew's palm. She stooped down to pick up a flat rock. Andrew was bouncing from one foot to another.

With a quick flick of her wrist, she swiped the rock against the bee and the stinger, removing both from his hand.

She looked into his face. "You allergic to bees?"

"I don't know," he grimaced.

"You don't know? What kind of reaction have you had to bees before?"

"I've never been stung before."

"What?" Tasha found that hard to believe. "Not even as a kid?."

He shook his head.

What a sheltered life, Tasha thought. She squeezed the flesh around the wound and scraped it again with the rock to make sure none of the stinger was left and to extract any of the poison.

"Yow!" Andrew jumped back and shook his hand away from her.

"Go wash it out in the lake," she told him.

"It will be all right." He examined it again.

"Go wash it out. At the very least the cold water might help keep the initial swelling down and wash some of the poison away."

When he returned, looking slightly less sheepish than before, Tasha had already decided what they needed to do. Wadding up the blanket he'd found, she approached him.

"It's getting late. We need to start back for the resort."

Andrew lifted one blond eyebrow at her. "But we have no—"

"Clothing, I know. I think we can stay off the beaten path as much as possible. I'm sure we can avoid the masses. Hell, Andrew, nudity is not such a big thing around here. If we stay in the trees, I think we'll be okay. And we can wrap this blanket about us if we run into anyone."

Andrew threw up his hands. "Oh, yeah. That wouldn't look suspicious at all, would it? People walk around wrapped in blankets all the time." He was obviously quite put out with the entire situation.

"You got any better ideas? I don't relish the idea of staying out here all night, particularly if those kids come back. I'm walking. You do what you want."

She gathered the blanket around her and headed for the dirt road leading away from the lake. She didn't dare look behind her.

Tasha stopped when she realized that they were about to come upon a clearing. After taking the dirt road away from the lake, they'd turned left onto something that looked like no more than a cow path and had ended up in a large overgrown area. Now there was a glimmer of light at the end of the tunnel—or at least at the edge of the woods.

Dusk fell slowly around them; the forest took on an eerie quality. Andrew shivered under his side of the blanket. Tasha glanced sideways at him.

"Sunburn giving you chills?"

"A little," he grumbled.

"Hand hurt?"

He thrust it between the blanket opening. "It's swollen," he grumbled again, then swiftly pulled it back under the blanket. Tasha watched as his side of the blanket started jerking around his abdomen.

"Bug bites?" she asked calmly.

Andrew stopped and turned a pained expression toward her. Slowly, his eyes closed. He took a deep breath and opened them again. "Yes, damn it! I've got chiggers or some kind of insect bites, okay? What the hell do you care?" He started scratching again.

Taken aback, Tasha simply looked at him. "Well, you don't have to be so grouchy. I was only inquiring."

He jerked the blanket and started walking again. Tasha had no choice but to follow. "Well, you can stop inquiring."

After a moment of studying him out of the corner of her eye, Tasha decided to risk it again. "I wasn't going to say 'I told you so,' you know. I was just going to say that when we get back to the room, I've got some stuff that will fix all of that."

Stumbling ahead, Andrew kept his gaze in front

of him. "Yeah, you're Little Miss Fix-it, aren't you?"

Again, stunned at his brusqueness, Tasha studied him. Then she stopped dead in her tracks. Andrew tried to continue on, but she jerked hard on the blanket, forcing him to stop and look at her.

"What's the matter with you, Andrew?" she asked, puzzled by his reaction to her questions.

When he faced her, she could see the worried lines in his face, the tautness of his features, could hear the impatience in his voice.

"You've got us lost, that's what. I'm damned tired of this. This whole entire hellish week has been something out of some insane Mel Brooks movie. I can't believe I'm stuck out here in the middle of no-man's-land with you, naked, no clothes, no glasses, lost, with an itching red body and a swollen"—Andrew cast his eyes about impatiently—"hand."

Tasha huffed out a quick breath and shook her head. "We're not lost. I had a map, remember?"

"But this isn't the way we came."

"No, I thought we'd try a short cut to keep us away from civilization. I really think we're right on target. There might be a short distance we'll need to travel closer to the road, but we'll get there, Andrew, and all in one piece."

He looked anywhere but her face. "You don't understand, do you?" he shouted at her.

"Understand what?"

"You don't understand what kind of a predicament I'm in here, do you?"

CRAZY FOR YOU 197

Confused and exasperated, Tasha dropped her shoulders in defeat, the corner of the blanket dipping down around her right breast, exposing the top of it. She watched Andrew's gaze fall to her chest, then heard his lips draw in a ragged breath.

"Andrew, yes, I understand. We're in this together. We'll get back to the resort and we'll buy you some new clothes. Now, stop worrying. Everything will turn out just fine."

Andrew's eyes clenched tight, then snapped open. Wild fury bolted out at her. "No! *No!* You don't *understand!* It's not we, it's *me*. I've got the problem here. Me, damn it!"

More puzzled than ever, Tasha sighed. "We're in this together."

"Together?" He laughed out loud. "I only wish."

Tasha dropped her arms further in exasperation, her eyes searching the trees above them; the blanket half exposing both her breasts.

"Damn!" Andrew jerked the blanket back up to her neck.

Tasha's mouth dropped open. "Andrew, I'm totally confused. I have no idea what's going on here."

"Okay. Then I'll tell you," he said in defeat. "Or, better, show you."

Jerking the blanket away, Andrew let it billow to the mossy earth. Silence prevailed around them for a moment and Tasha let her gaze fall to his hips. She gasped. His hand wasn't the only thing swollen.

"I'm horny as hell and embarrassed to death

someone other than you is going to witness my . . . predicament. I can't walk in there like this!" He pointed to his groin.

It was true. He was primed and ready. She bit her lip. Flashes of their earlier encounter on the dock spun through her mind. She should have realized the interruption wouldn't have stifled his desire for long. Obviously not even the short time they spent in the lake had. "Well," she said quietly, dragging her gaze from his engorgement to his pained face, "I think I can fix that, too."

Within milliseconds they were together. Andrew's lips crushed into hers as his palms framed her face. He threaded his fingers into the long tresses of her hair and pulled and tugged until their lips melded together as one.

Their hot, labored breaths came in short spurts as their lips and tongues frantically devoured chins and cheeks, ears and throats. Andrew dropped his hands from her face to her shoulders, then her breasts. His lips followed, and Tasha felt their warmth, their power over her as her body grew moist and languid.

She trembled, weak with the skill of his kisses and caressing hands. Her legs were going to collapse. She didn't think she could stand any longer. "Andrew . . ." she breathed.

They tumbled to the blanket that partially covered the mossy earth. Emotion reigned, catapulting her to another plane as Andrew's body slammed onto hers. His mouth slid down her chin; his hands cupped and kneaded the sides of her breasts. Urgently, he lowered his mouth to one nipple, then the other, suckling hungrily of her.

"Tasha . . . Tasha . . ." He spoke her name in coarse and ragged breaths against her heated skin. "I can't . . . I can't stand this much more."

Tasha could feel the hard pulse of him as his lips devoured her nipples and his throbbing masculinity ground into her near the juncture of her thighs.

"Let me fix it for you," she panted, reaching around him to grasp and pull low on his back, reaching down further to squeeze and pull at his buttocks. "Let me . . ."

Andrew raised his face to look at her, sliding forward to ensure a more perfect fitting of their bodies. His eyes never left hers as he lowered his mouth, savagely taking her lips with his. With the tip of his tongue, he urgently traced the outline of her mouth, then raked across her teeth, finally hurriedly parrying with her tongue, plundering her mouth as he soon would her body.

As Tasha's passion swelled within her, she arched upward, pulling his head closer to her, delving her tongue deep into his mouth. He reciprocated.

Then he broke the kiss and pulled away. Positioning his knees between her thighs, he kissed each of her breasts, then lower, just above her navel. Tasha felt the wild swirl of passion lick up inside her like flames. She wanted him. . . . now.

Grasping his shoulders, she pulled at him. "Andrew," she whispered. She couldn't stand it one more second. "I want you inside me. Now."

With a groan, Andrew dropped to her, supporting his weight on his elbows, and plunged deep inside her, satisfying the first of her primal needs—to be filled by him. She waited for the second—to be spun into oblivion as he rode her body there.

Fast and furious, they clung to each other, lips crashing into lips, hips into hips. His heat built deep inside her and she arched her body into his, meeting him thrust for thrust with wild abandon. He pushed and gave. She wanted and took. *Yes!* she screamed inside her mind. She wanted this and more. She wanted . . . him. She wanted. . . .

With his final thrust, Andrew slumped against her, cradling her to him. The dam burst inside her as well, fighting to put out the scorching flame inside. Slowly, slowly, the flame died, leaving her a mass of tingling, sensitive, fulfilled flesh.

Her eyes opened as Andrew lifted his face to look at her. With one hand raised to her cheek, he swept a stray hair out of her eyes and grinned at her. Tasha let her gaze play over his face for a moment, wondering what he was thinking.

"You okay?" he finally whispered to her. "That was kind of fast and hard."

She nodded. "I'm okay. You?"

He shifted off her to ease her of his weight. Gathering her close into him, he gently ran his fingers along her spine. "When we get out of this," he murmured into her hair, "I'm going to show you the other side of fast and hard."

"Oh, really?" Tasha cocked her head back to look at his face.

He dipped his head to kiss her. "Yeah," he growled against her lips. "The next time I'm going to be the one to do the fixing. And I'm an extremely slow but methodical worker. Sometimes I work late into the night."

Tasha grinned. "Then let's get out of here."

FOURTEEN

It was dark when they made it back to their room. Through the forest and under the veil of falling night, they stole along the paths that wound throughout the resort and entered the hotel.

Breathing a huge sigh of relief, Andrew dropped the blanket to the floor and plopped across the bed, taking Tasha with him. As they lay on their sides, looking at each other, Andrew threaded his fingers through Tasha's long tresses, their bodies heart to heart, their legs intertwined.

"Why don't you go take a shower?" Tasha quietly suggested. "I'll gather a couple of things together to take care of your injuries." She started to rise.

Andrew grasped her wrists and pulled her down to him. "Oh, no, you don't. I don't want you two inches away from me."

Tasha grinned. "Don't be silly. I'm just going to the dresser. Go take your shower!" Tasha broke away and playfully pushed him toward the edge of the bed.

"You come with me."

When the skin of their bodies touched, Tasha was sure electricity had passed through him and into her. She'd heard when a person was electrocuted, the electricity had to exit somewhere out of the body. She knew exactly where this bolt was going to end up sooner or later.

Her lips seared as his gently grazed hers. Her nipples tingled at their subtle raking over his chest. Her abdomen tightened when he pressed closer, her knees trembled, and her toes curled.

With her fingertips, she explored his neck and shoulder. The kiss deepened. Andrew wrapped his arms around her waist, groaned deep in his throat, and pulled her closer. Dragging his lips down her chin to her neck, he found the tiny pulse. She tossed back her head. He licked. Tasha's blood surged at the touch of his tongue there.

Taking in a ragged breath, she cradled his face in her hands and lifted her head up to look at him. "Andrew . . ." she dragged his name out on a wispy breath.

His eyes told her he understood. Breaking away, Andrew stood, still holding one of her hands, and pulled her off the bed toward the bathroom.

He efficiently adjusted the water temperature and started the spray. Tasha took in the firm muscles rippling across his back and tapering down to narrow hips. She noticed a mole on his right shoulder and a small scar under one rib as he turned back.

But when he looked at her, she saw something else entirely. His eyes were full of desire for her. They were full of caring and emotion. When he reached out and touched her, grasping her arm and pulling her into him, she felt it. Everything he was feeling poured out of him and into her. She knew the way Andrew made her feel was different from anything she'd ever experienced.

Even though it was emotion, more than physical desire or lust, that coursed through his body for her, she didn't care. She wanted it. It was the same stuff coursing through her body. More than anything, she needed to feel lost in the one thing she'd tried to avoid for years now—caring so deeply about someone that nothing else mattered.

For the moment, or for the next few hours or days, that's how it would be. She would lose herself in this, in Andrew. She wouldn't think about how he made her feel, she would just feel.

But she would not allow herself to love him. She couldn't. And she couldn't let him fall in love with her, either. They were two peas, different pods. Their worlds could never collide for long. They were only setting themselves up for major heartache if they let their feelings get too much in the way.

Andrew pulled her under the warm spray. As their bodies met in the small confines of the tiled shower, all thought flew out of her mind. There was no more reasoning to be done, no more thinking about what to do. There was no way brain activity could exist except for the cells that controlled pleasure, and they were going into overload.

His hands were all over her and she felt sweet surrender. Tasha's back was to the shower head;

the spray fell over her shoulders. Andrew had already lathered up handfuls of soap and had started at her neck, soaping her down. Tasha simply stood, her breathing shallow, her eyes closed, as he started at her shoulders, moved to her arms, lingered at her breasts, her tummy. He turned her and washed her back, tossing her long hair over one shoulder to the front, then slid his hands down to the curve of her tiny waist and the swell of her buttocks.

Again rotating her body toward him, he knelt as he continued down her thighs, taking both hands up and down the long length of her legs to her feet. Gradually, he returned to her inner thighs, then finally, he stood with another handful of soap, cupped her gently, and cleansed her where her legs joined.

Opening her eyes, Tasha found Andrew staring into her face. She smiled and he shot a slow grin back at her. "I sure hope that soap has natural ingredients in it," she murmured. "I never put anything in or on my body that's not natural," she teased.

Andrew growled and gently pushed her back under the shower spray to rid her body of all the soap bubbles. "Honey, anything I put on or in your body tonight will be all natural." He kissed her lips quickly and clasped her around the waist, tugging her closer to him as the spray bounced around their shoulders. "Don't you worry about that."

He turned her around then. "Let me wash your hair."

She glanced over her shoulder. "You don't have to. I can do it."

His eyes held hers. "I want to," he whispered.

Tasha turned back around. His fingers ran through her hair and every sensitive nerve ending in her scalp cried out in pleasure. He lathered shampoo into her hair, massaging her scalp and pulling it through to the ends of her waist-length tresses. Over and over again, he massaged and lathered. Tasha let her head drift back toward him. The caress of his fingertips as he rubbed in tiny circles and raked his fingernails gently across her scalp sent radiant spirals of sensation down her body to the tips of her toes.

"You have beautiful hair," Andrew whispered near her ear.

She let herself go, let herself simply feel.

He massaged behind her ears, and she tilted her head first one way then the other. He rubbed her neck and her body felt languid and lazy. He lifted and combed his fingers through her hair, and her body become so relaxed that she had to lean back against Andrew to support herself. He reached around and held her against him, his hand resting just under her breasts, his other still gently massaging her head.

The touch of his fingertips on her scalp was so erotically stimulating that she could feel it all over her body. Her pulse raced with the excitement building within her.

Thrusting one hand down over her abdomen to steady her, Andrew slid his hand lower and lower until he nestled his fingers in the small triangular patch of hair and gently caressed her. Pressing his fingers into her flesh, he forced her back firmly against him. Tasha could feel his own desire behind her, throbbing against her buttocks.

Then he released her and dipped her under the shower's spray again, thoroughly and quickly rinsing all the shampoo out of her hair.

Tasha turned to face him. "Your turn," she whispered.

He shook his head, his eyes full of determination. "No. Not yet."

He started at her breasts. First one nipple and then the other felt the assault of his lips and tongue. His hands braced her back as he quickly turned her and pushed her into the back wall of the shower. She fell into the wall, the palms of her hands flat against the tile. She didn't trust her limbs anymore to hold her body up, and with what he was doing to her now, she'd be just another puddle on the shower floor before long if she didn't have something to lean on.

His lips lowered. Trailing from just underneath her breasts down to her navel, he lovingly and caressingly kissed and licked, his rough tongue sending tremors up and down her body. Then he knelt in the shower before her, his hands flat against her abdomen, and slid lower.

He kissed down her left thigh and his hands followed the trail. Tasha lifted both her hands off the wall and cradled Andrew's head in them. Eyes closed, her head tipped back and her chest arched slightly forward as his left hand came up between her thighs and touched the sensitive flesh between her legs. Her breathing came in short gasps.

Andrew's lips rose up to her inner thigh, but stopped when he reached her feminine mound. Tasha sucked in a deep breath when his fingers spread her apart, then groaned his name as he planted his mouth at her center.

For a moment, they were simply joined that way. Tasha fought for control of her body, then felt herself slowly sliding down the shower wall.

Andrew caught her with his hands and pressed her back into the wall, his lips still on her. She moaned her pleasure as his tongue and mouth assuaged her throbbing need, for there were no words that could be said. This was something primal, basal, a physical act that went beyond words. He continued flicking with his tongue, laying the flat part against her, licking, creating and filling a part of her that had never been filled.

She felt the first quaking tremors deep within her. She was suspended somewhere between heaven and hell. The onslaught of pain and the pleasure he ravished on her body were somehow joined and a part of the other. The tremors increased and built within her. His hands kneaded her thighs as she pushed herself tighter against him. Gasping at his assault, she clutched his shoulders. With one final thrust against her flesh, she exploded into him. He gave and she took. She gave and he took. Again, her body went limp and slid.

Andrew stood and braced her against the wall with his body. Letting her head fall against his shoulder, he gathered her to him and cradled her close. With one hand, he gently massaged and caressed where seconds earlier he had loved her with his mouth, allowing her a slow entrance back to him.

Tasha thought she had somehow melted into him and wondered if she was even all there, still within her own body. Or was she a part of his? Ever since they'd made love . . .

Breaking the embrace, Andrew let her lean back against the shower wall again.

"The water's getting cool," he whispered into her cheek. "Stay there. I'm going to wash. Then we're going to finish this."

Leaning against the wall, Tasha watched as Andrew quickly lathered and soaped his body. Mesmerized, she watched his hands play over his face, his ribs and chest, his lips, down his thighs, and then quickly over his swollen genitals. Tasha felt a surge of passion rush through her. Even the cool water hadn't slowed him down, she mused, half smiling. He washed his hair, quickly lathering, then as his eyes closed and he dipped his head back under the shower spray, Tasha stepped forward and reached out, gently grasping his hardened shaft within her two hands.

Immediately, Andrew's gaze came up to meet hers. "Ah, honey, don't . . . not yet," he moaned.

But it was too late.

She knelt before him. Her sweet mouth was on him in a second. Every muscle in his body tensed at the tender invasion of her tongue. She ran her palms down his chest as she slid lower. Never before had he felt such passion, such a wild torrent of desire. Never before had a woman taken him like this. . . .

Her tongue slid down to the base of his shaft, then curled around him. When she dragged her hands down to his thighs and gently cupped him, he felt as if he'd died and gone to . . .

Then she devoured him.

"Sweet mother." He threaded his fingers in her hair and pulled her face up to look at him. "I'm cold . . ."

She arched an eyebrow at him. "You're cold?" she teased.

"No, damn it. I'm hot. Hell . . . you know I'm hot. The shower . . ." He could hardly stand, let alone put a complete sentence together. "Let's get out of here."

With a flick of his wrist he turned off the water. After stepping out of the shower, he encased Tasha in a huge fluffy towel and brought her to him. Slowly, he raked the towel over first her body then his, then let it drop to the floor as he kissed her lips.

Just outside the door, the bed waited. After a quick jerk of the covers, they fell into it.

They lay side by side for only a moment until Andrew could stand it no longer. Lifting himself up on one elbow, he partially covered her body with his. He smoothed a stray strand of hair away from her cheek, peered into her eyes as he trailed his fingertips along her jaw line, then over her lips. When they parted, he thrust his index finger inside. She closed her mouth over the end of it, much as she had done earlier at a point much lower on his body.

An ache surged inside him. Her eyes flared with need.

Andrew continued the trail down her body—neck, breasts, the small, smooth mound of her belly—and then lower until he touched her again where she most wanted him to—and he could tell she wanted him to. She arched into his hand and her eyelids fluttered at the touch. She sucked in a deep breath and let it out very slowly, moaning his name. Her body throbbed against him.

Andrew had watched each and every reaction his hands and lips had on her body, and it urged him on. He wanted the pinnacle. He wanted it all.

Quickly, he fully covered her, his body easing up on hers, meshing their heated warmth together. He kissed her, deeply, thoroughly, his tongue penetrating, invading her mouth, as hers did to him. He fought the urge to penetrate her in other ways. They panted and breathed of each other, tasted and devoured.

Tasha's hands kneaded his shoulders, clutching at his back, then lowering to his waist, his buttocks. He rocked against her and she broke away from the kiss, gasping for air as she bit into his shoulder. She slid both her hands between them, where his hips rocked into her pelvis, reaching, searching until she touched him. Her long finger scraped the engorged length of him and he shuddered.

"Be still," he commanded in a hushed whisper.

"Don't. Don't touch me." He gasped and eased off her, supporting his weight on his elbows. "I'm not going to last long, and I promised you slow and steady."

Smiling wickedly up at him, she grasped him again. The sensation of her long silky fingers over him nearly sent him reeling.

"I like fast and hard," Tasha taunted, her eyes sparkling with passion.

"You're a demon." He pushed her thighs apart with his knees.

"I know," she breathed and pulled his face down to hers.

Andrew thrust himself into the cradle of her thighs. Tasha cried out as he lifted her off the bed with the jolt of their joining. Again and again, he thrust into her deeper and deeper until he thought he'd drowned in her.

Again and again, she took him, wildly took him, to places he'd never been before. Their bodies played an unwritten tune, composed an impossible rhapsody, as their physical coming together shattered any myths of souls touching, flesh melding, one man and one woman cleaving together as one body.

Andrew knew it could not be a myth. It was all true, and making love with Tasha had proven it.

Tasha squeezed and tightened her body around him as he felt her giving way to passion's dance. One last thrust and he was deep inside her, filling her. He wanted to stay right there for a hundred years. There was no greater peace on Earth.

After a moment, he rolled off of her, gathered

her close to him and breathed in the mingled scent of their union. Her head lay against his beating heart. She'd flung her arm over his chest. He curled one of his legs over hers protectively and let her name escape from his breathless lips.

Then as Tasha relaxed further against him, he contentedly dozed, knowing for the last time in his life he had truly found love. After this, there could never be anyone else.

At Andrew's soft snore, Tasha lifted her head off his chest. She looked at him, his head back in relaxation, his lips partly open. He looked so content, so peaceful, so exhausted. They'd certainly had a day of it.

No, they'd had a week of it.

She gingerly lifted herself up on one elbow to look him more fully in the face, her eyes taking in every feature, every angle, every laugh line or jut of bone. She wanted to memorize every detail, remember every touch, recall every sensation for as long as she could.

For the first time in her life she felt whole, totally fulfilled. A part of him.

Panic gripped her heart.

She supposed it could be true—knew it *was* true. With a ragged sigh, she tore her gaze away from his face and buried it into his chest. Holding him close, she decided not to think about it any further tonight. She'd worry about it tomorrow.

She stayed there until she feared her salty tears would wake him, then rolled to the other side of the bed, clutched his pillow to her chest, and fell into an exhausted sleep.

FIFTEEN

Bittersweet awareness crept uneasily over Tasha as she awoke. She'd slept as if tied up in knots. Uncurling her tense body, she stretched to pull the kinks out of her back, legs, and arms, then slid her hands underneath her pillow and buried her face into it again as she slipped back into unconsciousness.

She dozed a little longer.

She was supposed to do something today, she knew, but her mind hadn't grasped it yet.

After a few minutes, her brain began to churn with activity and she realized it was morning. Light from the windows bathed her eyelids, causing them to flutter and finally open. Time to get up.

It took a few seconds to focus on the man lying beside her on the bed. Everything came rushing back to her.

Andrew was lying not ten inches away, his head propped on his bent elbow, watching her. She suspected he had been for quite some time.

Then she remembered what she had to do.

"Hi," she whispered, lying unmoving beside him.

"Morning." His gaze played over her face, his lips firm.

"Been awake long?"

Reaching over, Andrew picked up a strand of Tasha's hair. He let it slide between his fingers, then brushed the end along her cheek. "Long enough to watch you sleep and figure out a few things in the process."

A jolt of trepidation sliced through Tasha. *He's going to be the one to do it,* she thought. *He's going to end it now, so we can get it over with and forget. Like I could ever forget.*

"What things?" she asked meekly, almost afraid.

Andrew slipped his arm down to the bed and nestled his head on the pillow next to her. Pulling the sheet around them both, he settled in closer to her, his arm across her waist. Tasha moved so they could look directly into each other's eyes.

"You didn't sleep well."

"I was tired. I don't sleep well when I'm overly tired." *Liar. You only sleep lousy when something's on your mind.*

Andrew reached out and smoothed her forehead. "Your face was screwed up as tight as a ball of string when I woke this morning."

"I had a bad dream." *Liar. You never have bad dreams.*

"Oh? Tell me about it." His concerned eyes searched hers.

Tasha closed her eyes and shook her head. "I can't remember it," she said quietly.

"Something bothering you, Tasha?"

There it was—her out. He'd given it to her on

a platter. All she had to do was say, "Yes, something's bothering me. I have to go. Not just back home, but out of your life. I can't ever do this again." He was letting her off the hook.

She searched his eyes. He was waiting, daring her to say it—to end it all right there, cut the umbilical cord so they could go their separate ways. He wanted her to do it.

"No," she answered weakly, lying again. "There's nothing wrong." Everything was wrong.

In a heartbeat, Andrew smiled and rolled her over, flat on her back. He followed to cover her body with his. "Good. Because I have something very important to tell you. But first . . ." His lips captured hers in a sweet and urgent kiss, powerful and filled with deep emotion. He stirred her passion alive again as he had the night before.

Surprised, Tasha let her body get swept into Andrew's excitement. But her brain screamed at her to stop him.

He broke away, then lazily traced tiny circles at her temples with his fingertips as his gaze played over her face. Tasha watched his expression turn from intense longing to contented bliss to something she couldn't quite put her finger on.

Oh, God. No.

"I've been thinking," he said quietly, then planted another quick kiss at the base of her neck. "We've got one more day here and there's a lot to do. I'm going down to check on the bus thing in a while to see if Josh or Todd knows anything."

Tasha nodded. She had no idea where this was leading.

"While I'm gone, find your plane tickets so we can see if we're on the same flight back. If we're not, then I want to change mine."

"What?" she murmured just under her breath.

Andrew slid lower to place another kiss just over her left breast. Looking up, he continued. "We can talk on the plane and figure out what we're going to do. For a while, I guess, we can hop back and forth from Washington to Colorado, but that's going to get old, as well as expensive." He placed another kiss over her right breast.

Tasha shook her head in confusion. She brought her hands to his head and turned his face back up to look at her.

"What are you saying?"

He paused a moment. "I'm saying we need to get organized, make plans, figure out where our lives are going."

Just like the assiduous businessman would.

Stunned, Tasha dropped her hands to the bed. "Where *are* our lives going?" She felt the skin over her face tighten.

He leaned up then and rolled over to the side, grasping her waist to him, acting as if he didn't understand, didn't see how troubled she was. "Well." He rubbed his hand against the side of her breast. "I guess that's what we need to talk about."

Tasha's eyes widened and her chest heaved in one huge sigh. She broke away from him and sat up, facing him. "Andrew, I know where my life is going."

For the first time that morning, something that looked like fear rippled over his face. "Something *is* wrong, isn't it?"

Tasha closed her eyes and bit her lower lip. Sucking in a deep breath, she opened her eyes and looked at him. Myriad emotions twisted his features, the same emotions that tore through her heart. He knew.

Do it now.

"Andrew," she started softly, then reached out to touch his hand. "There will be no plans."

He stared at her, unmoving for a long moment. Finally, he blinked once, then took a deep breath. "I love you, Tasha," he said in a hushed voice. "You mean more to me than any woman ever has."

The words rushed and rippled over her skin, then buried themselves deep into her heart. She squeezed her eyes closed, forcing her tears to stay inside. "Don't," she whispered.

He reached out and took her hand. His touch sent her spiraling.

"Don't!" Tasha jerked back off the bed. Andrew still lay there, a questioning expression on his face. She looked away.

"Look at me, Tasha," his smooth voice commanded.

She couldn't and turned away. She didn't want him to see the tears. But he was behind her in a flash, grasping her arm, turning her to look at him. She didn't have time to wipe the tears away and couldn't look him in the eyes. Instead she stared into his chest.

"Look at me."

When she didn't, he grasped her chin and pulled it up so her eyes met his. "Look at me, damn it!" The raspiness of his voice undid her more than anything. She felt herself go limp. If his fingers hadn't been digging into her upper arms and chin, she would have fallen to the floor, she was sure.

"I said I love you. Don't tell me not to, Tasha, because I can't not love you. I love you! Simple as that."

With an extreme amount of self-control, Tasha forced herself to keep the connection with his eyes. "We've only had a few days together, Andrew. One night, really. How can you say that you love me? There hasn't been enough time."

"I've had all the time I need. I know I love you."

Her heart slammed against her chest wall. She couldn't look into his eyes any longer. Forcing her arms out of his grasp, she backed away from him. "Well, I haven't had enough time."

"I'll give you all the time you need. Then I want you to marry me."

Horror raced through her heart.

Marry him?

She shook her head. "Impossible! I can't live in Seattle, Andrew. I don't do well in cities. Besides, I wouldn't fit into your world."

"Then I'll live in yours," he countered quickly.

This was going way too fast. "No. I mean, you

wouldn't be happy there, either, Andrew. I live in the middle of nothing. What would you do there? You couldn't sell pharmaceuticals, that's for sure. Hell, I sell more medicinal treatments in my shop than the drugstore down the road does. There's not a hospital within a hundred miles. It wouldn't work."

"Then I'll find another job."

Exasperated, Tasha turned away from him and rubbed her hands over her face. When she looked back over her shoulder at him, she saw a determined man, a strong man, set in his ways—traditional male, home, hearth, family. As much as she wanted to fling herself in his arms, she knew she couldn't. She couldn't give him what he needed, what he wanted, what he was accustomed to in his life.

She could never give him the picket fence.

It wasn't in her, never would be, and she knew it. She had to accept it and get on with her life.

Even if she loved him back.

Icy shards broke loose within her soul, causing her to shiver. She loved him back.

I do love you, Andrew.

All the more reason to let him go.

"No." She turned and started to gather up her things. "There's not enough time to make this work."

"I don't mean this week, Tasha. I mean after we leave here. I'll give you all the time you need." He crossed the room to her, grasping her hand.

Tasha jerked away and glared at him. He didn't understand! He couldn't just push his way into her life. There was too much to consider, too much that would have to change. She didn't want her life to change. Did she?

Confused rage built inside her. Anger might be the only thing that would get her through this, she thought. It was the only emotion she could grasp at the moment, so she went with it.

Tasha lit into him. "A lifetime wouldn't make this work, Andrew! I *told* you this couldn't happen. Remember? I told you a few days ago that after this week is over, there is no *us,* that it didn't matter what happened, whether we made love or fell in love, it couldn't leave this place." She straightened to her full height and felt the fury building within her. "This is not real. It's a fantasy. I'm going to go home and so are you, and we're not going to give each other another thought. Understand?"

"And you can honestly do that?" Andrew stood surprisingly calm in front of her. "I remember it all perfectly well, Tasha. I've been up half the night thinking about it. You're wrong. This isn't fantasy. This is real. What we shared is real. And for the record, you didn't say anything about falling in love. You simply said if we made love. There's a difference."

"No." She backed away again, jerked the sheet off the bed and wrapped herself up in it. "It never happened, Andrew. It's for the best."

"Why are you so frightened of admitting you feel something for me, Tasha? Why can't you tell me you love me? You more or less just admitted it. Why can't you say the words?"

"I'm not frightened."

"Then why don't you look me in the eye? Why are you crying?" His voice rose in anger and Tasha cringed. "Why are you suddenly wrapping yourself up in that sheet? Don't you want anyone but me to see you naked anymore?" After a moment, she felt his hand on her shoulder, and her body shuddered with a sob. "Why?" he whispered again.

She spun around to face him. This time she didn't care if he saw her tears. It didn't matter. Nothing was going to change what she had to do. "Why? I should think it would be obvious, Andrew. We're total opposites. Our lives would never mesh. You know I couldn't exist in your world and you couldn't exist in mine. You'd work all the time and I wouldn't have anything to do. We'd fight, we'd disagree, and we'd ruin what we had here this week.

"You're prime rib and I'm tofu. You wear boxer shorts and most of the time I wear nothing at all. You harbor the all-American dream. I abhor it. You're a fine Bordeaux and I'm homemade apple wine. We'd argue politics and religion, how to raise our kids, and how to treat their illnesses. And the worst part is we'd come to hate each other."

Looking into his troubled face, Tasha exhaled, releasing all her pent-up emotion. "I couldn't stand that."

Andrew took a moment to digest what she'd said. Tasha waited, expecting him to buck all her theories, but he didn't. "I never thought you were the kind to give up so easily."

Feeling her eyes narrow, she shook her head slightly at him. "I'm not."

"Then why are you doing this?"

"Because it's for the best."

"For you? Or are you doing this because you think it's best for me?"

She glanced away. "It's best for both of us."

Taking her chin in his hand again, he forced her to look at him. His voice was soft, calming, but his words held a venom that frightened her. "Tell me you don't love me, Tasha. Say the words. Then I'll leave here and forget all of this. I'll forget you. Otherwise, I'll never believe you don't want me. Until I hear the words, I will never give up hope."

The words were there, on the tip of her tongue, but she couldn't retrieve them.

I don't love you, Andrew. I don't, she wanted to cry out. But the words stuck in her mouth like wallpaper paste. Her tongue was dry, numbing her ability to speak, and she wanted more than anything to say the words to him. She knew it would cause him momentary misery, but it was better than ruining his life.

But it was a lie. She did love him.

Tears spilled onto her cheeks. Finally, pulling free from his grasp, she leaned into the door. Breathing heavily, she stared at him for another moment.

"Give it some time, Tasha," he urged. "I'm begging you, give us some time. I'll leave you alone all day if you want. I'll sleep on the roll-away tonight. You can think about everything I've said, everything you've said. Then tomorrow we can discuss this rationally. Please, Tasha, don't give up on us before you've had time to think it through. Give it one more day."

Tasha searched his pleading face. She didn't have the heart to hurt him any further. She couldn't. Gathering up her sheet, she stepped back into the room, her gaze level with his as she neared the bed. At the last minute, she broke away, curled up into a fetal position on the bed, and closed her eyes.

"All right," she whispered. "I'll give it one more day."

Throughout the remainder of the day and night, Andrew planned his strategy. Time. She needed time to adjust to all this. He would give it to her.

Sometime after midnight as he lay in bed, he recalled her frightened and confused face. It had been too much, too soon. He shouldn't have thrust his ideas upon her like that. It would be a major adjustment. Maybe she wasn't up to it yet.

Time. She needed time. That was the key.

He'd given her the day. He'd give her the night, too. He'd use the time to make some plans, but come morning, their last day together, he had a lot of other work to do. He had to work on her.

They weren't going to leave this place without making some sort of game plan. He wouldn't allow that to happen, mainly because of one simple factor: She couldn't say she didn't love him.

And tomorrow, he was all set to prove to her she did love him. His heart pounded at the thought of hearing her say the words.

He wasn't going to live the rest of his life without her. Whether she believed him or not, he would do whatever it took—moving, finding another job, eating her damned tofu. He would do it.

He loved her that much.

SIXTEEN

The tail end of a gauzy curtain whipped against Andrew's face, waking him. The cool breeze was welcome. The past few days and nights had been so hot. Groggy, he turned in the roll-away as he heard a knock at the door. Glancing to his right, he searched the king-size bed for Tasha's form beneath the covers, wondering if she would get up to answer it.

The knocking persisted.

Puzzled, Andrew got up and made his way toward the door, still eyeing the unmade bed. He glanced to the door of the bathroom, which stood ajar. It was dark beyond. She wasn't in there.

Maybe she'd taken an early walk.

Andrew pulled open the door and faced a smiling Josh.

"Came to tell you the bus strike is over. The next bus out leaves in an hour."

Andrew stared at him. Four days ago he could have kissed Josh directly on the lips. Now he didn't feel the least bit ecstatic. He reached out and shook the man's hand. "Thanks, Josh. Thought I'd never hear those words."

"Just thought you'd want to know."

CRAZY FOR YOU

"Appreciate it, man." Andrew glanced back again at the empty bed. Where was Tasha?

Turning back, he scratched his head and looked into Josh's eyes. "You didn't happen to see Tasha this morning, did you?"

Josh eyed him. "I did."

Andrew sighed. "Meditating with Samuel again?"

He shook his head.

"Must have taken an early walk, then."

Josh still stared blankly at him.

A slice of panic gripped Andrew's heart. "Where did you see her, Josh?"

After clearing his throat and glancing quickly at the ground, Josh replied, "She left early this morning on the first bus."

"Left on the bus?" Andrew tried not to panic.

Josh nodded his head and looked into Andrew's eyes. "Yes. Had her bags with her and hightailed it outta here. Looked in a mighty big hurry, to boot."

Stunned, all Andrew could do was stare dumbfounded into Josh's face. His heart swelled, filled with something he could barely define, and he thought it would burst.

Fear, that was it. He was scared to death. He couldn't breathe. An ache so deep and intense it nearly knocked him off his feet slammed into his chest.

Tasha's gone? No!

He searched the suddenly stifling room. There was no place to hide anything. He went to the one closet and thrust open the door.

Empty.

His mind reeled. No backpack. No carry-on. No Tasha.

Frantic now, he whirled about looking for anything that might give him a clue. Something concrete. How could he have been so stupid?

Clues. He needed clues.

He didn't know the name of the town she lived in, did he?

What was the name of her shop?

Her parents. He couldn't very well look up Zeus and Violet Rainbow in the phone book, could he? And how many damned Smiths, T. could there be in the state of Colorado anyway? Or would it be Smith, M.?

How was he going to find her?

Andrew fell flat against the bed and dragged his hands over his face in defeat. He would not give up. He loved her, damn it, and she loved him. He would find her.

Wearily, he sat up and glanced to his left at the bedside table, and there he saw a piece of resort stationery folded in half like a tent, leaning against the lamp. His name was scribbled across the front.

Finally, taking a deep breath, he picked it up. The chatter in his brain fell silent. With his forefinger, he unfolded the note.

Dear Andrew . . .

Coward.
The word had echoed and bounced inside her

brain since she'd stolen away from the resort in the middle of the night. She'd waited in the lobby for almost two hours, thinking she'd be there to bum a ride from someone very early in the morning. Then a bus magically appeared.

She'd given Andrew what he wanted—one more day. He'd left her alone. She'd found out later he'd spent the day at the beach—sunning and thinking, he'd told her. Making plans was more like it. It seemed Andrew was getting all his ducks in a row. They were cordial to each other at night. Each had gone to a separate bed and quietly told the other good night.

Tasha had lain quiet and still until she heard Andrew's even breathing. When he was deeply asleep, it was simple enough to slip her backpack from underneath the bed and escape, even though it pained her heart to do so.

With each rotation of the bus's wheels taking her further away from Andrew, the word screamed out at her.

Coward! Coward!

She knew she was.

She'd breathed one huge sigh of relief when she'd boarded the plane in Montego Bay without any interference from Andrew. The remainder of the trip, from Miami to Dallas and then Dallas to Denver, she managed to sleep—somewhat.

Now, as she rolled down the window of her old Toyota pickup truck to pay her long-term parking bill at the airport, she heard the word again.

Coward.

She'd cried nearly the whole trip home. Every

time she closed her eyes, she saw him. Everything she touched reminded her of him. And with every mile further she drew away from him, her heart fell a little closer to the ground.

She felt separated—disjointed, as though she'd been taken apart at the seams, one half of a whole.

Part of her soul was missing.

But she'd had to do it. She'd had to leave Andrew. There was no other way. The break had to be clean and quick. If she'd held on any longer, she might not have been able to do it.

"Mark's on the phone again." Violet covered the mouthpiece of the receiver with the palm of her hand as she whispered the words to Tasha. She'd only been home three days, but Mark had called at least twice each day. It didn't take long for news to get around this small town. Her mother thrust the phone toward Tasha. "Talk to him," she urged.

Tasha met her mother's gaze, then quickly shook her head. Turning her back to her mother, she crossed the shop toward a case of Indiana cantaloupe she'd just had shipped in. She heard her mother's exasperated sigh, then her muffled reply to Mark.

God, I'm gutless.

The receiver clicked in the cradle.

"Moontasha, that's the last time I'm going to do that."

Tasha fumbled through the melons, hearing

every word her mother said, but acting as if she didn't.

Her mother was not to be ignored this time, though. Stepping up beside her daughter, she stilled Tasha's hands and pulled them to her. Tasha finally looked her mother in the face as she turned.

"Do you understand what I'm saying? That boy is hurting. You owe it to him to speak to him. You have to be able to explain what happened, why you called off the wedding. Tasha, I never thought you a coward before, but you're acting pretty much that. You've got to snap out of it and face the music, honey!"

Tasha sucked in a deep breath and held it for a moment as she looked off to the right. Couldn't her mother see there was much more than Mark Tasha had to deal with? Couldn't she see her daughter was hurting, too?

In the next instant, she expelled the breath and her eyes misted over. "I know I hurt him, Mama." She choked back the tears. "But I can't talk to him yet. I've got some other things to deal with. I just can't seem to get it together."

"You went to that resort to get yourself together so you could talk to Mark. Why haven't you done that yet?"

Tasha met her mother's gaze again as tears slipped over her lower lids. A flash of recognition crossed her mother's face, and Tasha knew her mother was somehow figuring things out. She'd avoided talking to her about the trip and about Andrew. It was too soon. She wasn't ready to analyze what had happened between them. But her mother was too damned perceptive. She'd never been able to keep secrets from her.

"You met someone."

After a moment, Tasha nodded.

"And you feel guilty after leaving Mark just a short time ago."

Tasha nodded again.

"Are you in love with him?"

Closing her eyes, Tasha responded, "Yes."

"And you don't know how you're going to tell Mark. You fled your own wedding six weeks earlier to a man you've cared about since you were a child, and now, a short time later, you've fallen in love with someone else. Are you in the least concerned how Mark is going to take this?"

Opening her eyes to peer into her mother's face, Tasha held her breath a moment before answering. She shook her head. "No," she replied softly. "I'm not worried about how Mark is going to take this. Mark will never know."

"Tasha, that's cruel." Her mother's tone was rising. She almost never raised her voice to Tasha. "Mark deserves to know you've fallen in love with another man. He deserves to know the truth."

"No, he doesn't, Mama. Mark will never know, because I'm never going to see Andrew again. I love him, but I'm never going to see him again. I'm not going to hurt Mark any more."

At the surprised look on her mother's face, Tasha stepped away and headed for the back room of the shop. Right now, she didn't feel like disappointing another person in her life. She'd disappointed too many already—including herself.

"Damned necktie."

Andrew ripped it from his shirt collar and tossed the lavender and lime green striped scrap of fabric at the passenger seat of his car. Ever since he'd left Jamaica, the damned things seemed to grip his throat like a noose.

Sighing, he raked a hand through his hair and glanced into the rearview mirror. He'd needed a haircut three weeks ago. Stopping at a red light, he squinted into the mirror again. Actually, he kind of liked the look. It wasn't as rigid.

Someone honked behind him. Traffic raced forward on either side. Andrew pressed the accelerator and glanced at his appointment pad attached to the dashboard. He was late for his three-thirty. Damn. He screeched to another halt as the light turned red in front of him.

Agitated, he drummed his fingers on the steering wheel. The light changed and he lurched forward. Three-forty-seven. His cell phone rang. Grasping it, he flipped the switch.

"Powell."

"Need your sales figures, Powell." It was Doug Johnston.

"I'll have them on your desk in the morning."

"I need them now."

Andrew blew out a breath. "Look, Johnston. I'm late for my three-thirty. You'll get them in the morning."

"Mayes wants them now."

"Well, he'll have to wait." Andrew cut him off.

The car directly in he front of his screeched to a halt. Andrew braked, narrowly missing its taillight. The driver threw him an obscene gesture. A sharp pain lanced across his chest and Andrew winced as he rubbed the soreness away.

Abruptly, he made a right hand turn and pulled over to the curb. He sat in the parked car for quite a while, staring out the windshield in front of him. Suddenly his three-thirty didn't matter anymore. There were two questions on his mind. They'd plagued him for the past few weeks.

How had he stayed in this job for so long? And how was he going to live the rest of his life without Tasha?

He'd just about given up finding her.

He'd give up just about anything to have his crazy nut back.

"Here, child. Mama's brought you some tea."

Tasha glanced up as her mother came steadily across the shop, a steaming brew in the delicate china teacup she offered. Curling her legs beneath her in the window seat, Tasha took the tea and set it down on the rough wood, then gazed back out the window to watch the small-town activity.

Violet sat in the rocker beside the window. She tucked the newspaper she'd been reading between her leg and the chair. "Aren't you going to try it?"

"What is it?" she asked, not really caring. She'd drink it—eventually.

"Valerian."

"Oh." Tasha's gaze drifted back to her mother. "Do you think I need a sedative or something?"

Smiling, Violet leaned forward. Her long, flowing dress bunched around her ankles as she reached over to clasp Tasha's hands. "You haven't slept well in weeks, honey." Her mother's eyes sparkled at her. "You can't deny this any longer. What you need to do is drink that tea, let it give you a good night's sleep, then get up in the morning and deal with this problem of yours."

Sighing, Tasha slipped her hands from her mothers' and turned back to the view out the window. She hadn't been any good to anyone in weeks, and she knew it. Her mother was practically running the store, and Tasha hadn't been outside in so long her skin was pale and sallow. Her customers made comments, but Violet stayed quiet most of the time. Tasha figured she'd just about had enough.

Outside, the sun was ready to slip over the mountain behind the town, bright with the colors of fall. It was beautiful, and normally she would have been out there in it. But she felt more black and white than anything. She didn't need to be a part of the kaleidoscope outside.

She didn't want to be cheered up. She didn't deserve it.

"No," she whispered, then turned back to face her mother. "There's no dealing with anything, Mama. You've heard it all. I ran out on Andrew.

He's not going to want me. Even if he did, he's so different from us, you and Daddy and me. He wouldn't fit into this world. I wouldn't fit into his world. There's nothing to discuss."

Her mother didn't hesitate to respond. She clasped her daughter's hands again and looked directly into her eyes. "Do you love Andrew, Tasha?"

She felt the tears sting her eyes as soon as her mother said the words. She nodded. "Yes," she breathed. "Oh, Mama, I love him so."

Her mother's face dipped in acknowledgment with one quick nod. Tasha knew advice was forthcoming. It had been a long time.

"Tasha," Violet began quietly, "you seem to have a history of difficult relationships. You tried to have something with Mark and that was all wrong. But you have to remember all that is in your past. Don't let something good slip out of your fingers because you're afraid of what might happen in the future. It's a risk we all have to take from time to time. You have to decide if the risk is worth taking. If it is, then go for it. If it's not, then pick yourself up and go on with your life.

"You've been hurt and you've been the one to do the hurting. Both of those situations are painful. Which are you frightened of this time?"

Tasha met her mother's gaze. "I'm not sure."

"Then what is it?"

"I don't want him to change because of me. I don't want to ruin his life."

"What if he doesn't think it's ruining his life?

What if that's what he wants? What if you're what he needs?"

Tasha glanced to her lap and shook his head. "I don't think I'm what he needs."

"Is that what he says?"

Again, Tasha shook her head.

"Don't be afraid to make a world of your own, Tasha. Go to Andrew. Tell him you love him. Make a world of your own, the two of you. Take the risk."

Her mother stood and Tasha pointed her tear-filled face to the window. It was just like her mother to search for the plain truth and the simplest answer.

Make a world of your own.

Take the risk, if it's worth it.

Andrew is worth it.

Stricken with sudden realization, Tasha turned back to her mother. "Oh, Mama, what am I going to do? I don't even know how to find him. All I know is he works in some pharmaceutical firm in Seattle!"

"Drink the tea, go to bed, then deal with it in the morning, child. And remember this: Your father and I made our world. We don't expect it to be yours. Do what you have to do. Somewhere out there your future is waiting. Who knows, you could end up right back here or you could end up across the world. But whatever happens, you have to make it happen. If you want to live your life with Andrew and he wants that, too, then the two of you will find a way." She rose and started for the door. "But first, there's something else you need to take care of."

Puzzled, Tasha glanced away for a second, then back to her mother. "And what is that?"

"Before you can go on with your life, I think there's a little matter from the past which needs to be addressed."

Tasha looked into her mother's eyes and nodded. She knew what she had to do. "When did you become so wise?" she whispered.

Violet smiled. "When you came into my world and made me that way.

SEVENTEEN

A dizzying sense of déjà vu gripped Tasha as she stepped up the stone walkway to Mark's house. Hidden behind a stand of trees and tucked into a small cranny above Pinebow Springs, the house had always been a welcome refuge. As a child, Mark had lived here with his parents. His parents had chosen a smaller, more convenient home for themselves and had sold Mark the large cabin a few years ago. When Tasha and Mark would play together as children, she used to ride her bike up the incline drive to greet him. From there, they always got into loads of trouble.

Mark was special to her. She could tell all her secrets to him. She could talk to him about things she couldn't tell anyone else. They shared almost everything, except intimacy. They'd both had other lovers over the course of their adult years, but she and Mark had never made love. Maybe it was because they both knew it wasn't right between them in that way.

Suddenly, a pang pierced Tasha. If Mark loved her as deeply as he claimed, why hadn't he pushed it all these years? Why hadn't she realized it was unusual for a man not to pursue sex with the woman he claimed to love? Why hadn't Mark ever mentioned it?

They had kissed, hugged, even touched intimately, but it had never gone any further.

She stepped on the porch and the door to the cabin opened before she took the second step. All her previous thoughts dissipated when she saw him. Mark stood on the threshold, staring at her. After a moment, he simply said her name.

Tasha found the courage to step forward. "I need to talk to you."

He nodded. "I need to talk to you, too." He motioned for her to come inside.

Tasha crossed the room. Mark followed and asked her to sit down. She settled herself in a huge sofa of southwest design. Mark pulled an ottoman closer and sat directly in front of her. She watched his eyes as he sat. They never broke the connection with hers.

Quickly, almost hesitantly, he reached out and grasped both her hands. Tasha welcomed the familiarity of his touch.

"Tasha," he began, his voice raspy, "we have to be honest with each other."

She nodded and continued watching his face.

"And I think maybe it will make things a little easier if I go first."

Tasha slid to the edge of her seat and grasped his hands a little tighter. "No, Mark. Please, let me. I need—"

Mark broke in. "We both need to get some things off our chests. We've needed to talk for weeks."

Finally Tasha tore her gaze from his. Her eyes played over the beamed ceilings, the dark paneled walls, and the thick, heavy furniture of the room. All of these things were so familiar to her, just like Mark. How could she break his heart? How could she live her life without his friendship? For surely, when this conversation was through, he wouldn't want to have another thing to do with her. What would she do without him in her life? She didn't know if she could fathom that.

She brought her gaze back to him and somehow found the courage deep inside to speak. "I'm ashamed of myself, Mark. I've avoided you for too long. It was just"—she glanced away momentarily and then back—"it was just that I suddenly realized I couldn't go through with it. Mark, you are my closest friend. You have been for years. I love you with all my heart. But as much as I hate to say this, I don't love you the way I should to marry you. I've known it for a long time. I just couldn't say it to you, couldn't bring myself to disappoint you. I just . . . I just . . . couldn't."

Tasha didn't realize she was crying until Mark reached up and swiped his forefinger across her cheek, removing her tears. As his gaze penetrated hers, she lowered her head onto both their hands and sobbed. "I'm so sorry I h-hurt you. I care for you s-so much. I don't know what I'm going to do without you."

Mark slipped from the ottoman to sit beside her on the couch. He cradled her in his arms and held her as she cried. He soothed her with comforting words and smoothed her hair back out of her face with his hands until she quieted and sat up to look at him.

"Please don't hate me. I don't think I could stand that."

Mark took a deep breath and held it. Finally, he exhaled. "Tasha, I haven't been completely honest with you, either. I want you to listen to me."

Tasha searched his face and saw the pain etched across it. He continued. "One of the reasons I was so desperate to talk to you was because I wanted to tell you I understood. You're right, we're not lovers. We're not in love. We have a special relationship that will last a lifetime, but we should never have attempted marriage. I guess I felt the biological clock ticking away. I hadn't found anyone who measured up to my standards except you. Finally I realized I was measuring every woman I dated to you, because I think you're one helluva woman. I care deeply for you. But, Tasha, I don't love you, either. Please forgive me for pushing you into this marriage idea. For months I had visions of children and the two-car garage and a fantasy of a life I still might have someday. But we both know it won't, and shouldn't be, for us. Not together."

Stunned, Tasha lowered her gaze to find both their hands now in their own laps. It was as if they'd both let go. They could stand on their own two feet now. Suddenly, Tasha felt exuberant. It was as though every grain of guilt had washed away with the last of her tears. "Oh, Mark. We've fooled ourselves for so long, haven't we?"

Smiling slightly, he nodded. "Yes, I think we have. But, Tasha, it will happen for each of us. We'll each find someone to be happy with and to love. And when that happens, it won't be forced and contrived. It will be true love."

At that, the tears welled up in Tasha's eyes again. She had to go on, had to finish what she'd come here today to do. She nodded in agreement with him. "I've already found someone, Mark. I met someone."

"And you love him?"

"Yes."

"Then what are you doing here?"

Tasha couldn't think of a reason. Everything was said; it was time for her to go. Why wasn't she with Andrew? "I don't know. I guess I needed to see you first, to make my peace with you."

"Go, Tasha. Go be with the one you love."

Nodding, Tasha rose. Mark stood also. Hesitantly, she reached out and pulled him into her embrace. "Thank you," she whispered.

Mark held her for a moment and then released her. With his hand, he cupped her chin and held her face close to his for a few seconds longer. "Be happy, Tasha. And never forget I'll always be here for you."

Nodding, the tears returning, Tasha gave him one last, brief hug, then slipped out of his embrace and left the cabin.

* * *

Andrew slapped the papers down against his desk and smiled. It was a done deal. After weeks of everything in his life going wrong, something was finally going right.

At the very least, he'd been determined. He'd set goals and put his analytical mind to work, just as he'd done in every other aspect of his life. He'd pushed emotion away and concentrated solely on the tasks at hand. He tried all the obvious things first—the phone, tracing the airline ticket, inquiring at the resort—but without luck. He'd faced a roadblock at every turn.

So he'd developed a plan:

A. Find Tasha
B. Make love to her until she is either convinced or too exhausted to fight.

It was that simple.

But in case that didn't work, he also had Plan B. He hadn't quite worked out all his strategy for that one yet, but he was damned close. Closing the real-estate deal today was the first step. He just needed her cooperation.

The problem was there was no guarantee it would work. Well, he'd just have to keep his hopes up. He would never give up.

He'd lost out most of his adult life because he'd put relationships on hold due to business. He'd be damned if he'd waste any time building a life with Tasha. He'd wasted time with Diana. He wouldn't make that same mistake again.

Leaning back in his chair, he let his head fall

back and his eyes close. Every time he did that he saw her, eyes flashing, hair billowing out about her as they swam that day, then later, as they made love in the rain forest. The ache in his heart tried to take over, but he wouldn't let it, not until he saw her. Then he'd let it pour out of him.

He pushed it all aside and sat erect in the chair. Reaching up, he straightened the red, green, and purple tie at his neck. He was restless. He had to get out of here.

Then again, he had only two more weeks to go until he kissed this place good-bye forever. He stood to go. Before he left, though, he reached over and flipped open the tattered piece of stationery he kept tucked into his desk pad and read the note one more time, as he did several times each day. At times, it was the only thing that kept him going.

Dear Andrew,
I know I'm doing the wrong thing by leaving like this, but I'm frightened. I couldn't say the words last night because they wouldn't be true. I don't want to ruin your life. We could never make it together. Don't love me, Andrew. Find someone else to love you. Find someone else to give you that picket fence. You would never be happy with me in the end.

Love,
Tasha

"You're wrong, Moontasha Begonia Smith." Andrew stared past the note for a moment, then folded it and tucked it back in the corner of the deskpad. "I will be very happy with you for the rest of my life. And I'm going to prove that to you very soon."

Tasha adjusted the jacket of her navy suit, then bent to flick a piece of grass from her new navy pumps. Glancing up, she read the signboard over the flight desk to check on her flight. No news. There was a problem with the plane and she was going to have to lay over in Portland for another hour or more.

She leaned back into her seat. It had been a long day. She was ready to get to Seattle, check into her hotel room, and start the search for Andrew. She didn't know the name of his firm, but she figured she could call every pharmaceutical company in the book until she found the one that employed him.

That would be the easy part.

The hard part would be facing him once she found him. But it was something she had to do, even if he told her to turn around and head back to the mountains. At least then she would know.

She'd gone shopping the day before. The suit and pumps had felt uncomfortable at first, but she was getting used to them. Her mother had laughed, then hugged her. It was her first attempt to fit into Andrew's world. Maybe it wouldn't be as difficult an adjustment as she originally thought.

A hunger pang stabbed at her belly.

Rising, she spotted a food stand. She had plenty of time to grab something. Maybe she should do it now.

She ordered a ice water and took a sip while she waited for her sandwich. After a minute, she took the small bag from the young boy behind the counter and turned back to the waiting area.

She took another sip of the water and plowed into the man standing behind her.

"Oh, excuse me." She glanced blindly at him. The only thing she noticed was the Co-Ed Naked Volleyball shirt he was wearing.

Wait a minute. Was that a Club Regale Co-Ed Naked Volleyball T-shirt?

"That's all right."

Tasha stepped back. The voice was familiar. She looked up into his face.

The hair was longer, mussed. The T-shirt, denim shorts, and Nike basketball shoes were quite different from what she was used to seeing him wear. He looked infinitely more relaxed.

But it was *him*. Her insides wanted to melt into a puddle right there on the floor. Good vibes were spinning webs around her.

Standing right before her, smiling, was Andrew.

"I spotted you from across the way. I hardly recognized you." Andrew reached out and flicked at her lapel. "Nice threads."

Amazed, Tasha cleared her throat. "Yeah." She touched his chest. "Yours, too. What are you doing here?"

Glancing briefly away, Andrew shrugged. "Catching a plane to Denver."

"Why?"

"I've got a new job there."

Tasha swallowed. "In Denver?"

He shook his head. "No, actually it's outside of Denver. Small town called Pinebow Springs. Ever heard of it?"

Tasha's heart leapt. "Yes."

"It's different from what I did before, but I think I can handle the position."

"Oh?"

"Ummmmm."

"And what is the position?" She couldn't think of a thing in Pinebow Springs she could see Andrew doing. Had her mother had a hand in this?

"I bought a small farm there."

"A farm?"

"Yeah. It was the weirdest thing. There was this real-estate ad in my mailbox one day, mailed in a plain white envelope, no return address. But it was postmarked Pinebow Springs. Know anything about it?"

Tasha closed her eyes. Her mother? Mark? Were they in cahoots? She opened them again. "I wish I did. I wouldn't have had the guts to do that."

"You had the guts to get this far."

The thought stung her. She had, hadn't she?

"What are you going to do with a farm, Andrew?"

"Oh, I don't know. Grow some vegetables. Some herbs. Raise a cow or two, maybe some chickens. Probably end up with a whole passel of kids someday. I've been doing some research

Tasha laced her arms around his neck and leaned forward for another kiss. "How much longer? When we get back to Pinebow Springs?"

"Uh-uh. I think we should spend one last night in the city before we head to the country. Ever spent the night in Portland?"

Tasha shook her head. "No."

"First time for everything, they say."

"That's what I hear."

"Then let's set the damned town on fire."

"Or at least the hotel bed."

"Tasha!" Andrew's face registered surprise.

"Well, we've got to get started on that passel of kids sometime, don't we?"

Nodding, Andrew linked his arm in hers and pulled her into the flow of the crowded airport. *One thing's for certain,* she thought, *we will definitely produce interesting children.*

"Darling, you can get rid of every stitch of clothing you possess."

Smiling wickedly, Tasha took off her jacket and pulled her cotton shirt from the waistband of her skirt.

Andrew pulled her close and kissed her lips. "Not now, honey. Later."

Tasha laughed, then grew serious. "I have to say this, Andrew, just this one thing. I'm sorry I left you the way I did. I just didn't think we—" He silenced her with one finger on her lips.

"There are only three words I want to hear from you right now. Later, we can sort out all the rest."

Tasha knew the words by heart. She'd practiced them since she'd left Colorado. "I love you, Andrew."

He smiled, then captured her lips with his. "That's four words," he teased between kisses.

"I know, but I'm not counting, are you?"

Andrew sighed. "The only thing I'm counting on is keeping you naked and natural for some time to come, sweetheart. Maybe barefoot and pregnant, too."

Smiling wickedly, Tasha agreed. "I can live with that. When do we start?"

Andrew caught her lower lip between his teeth. "I'm ready whenever you are," he teased, then nibbled at both her lips.

Tasha pressed into him. "That's apparent," she whispered back between grinning kisses.

"But I think we'll have to wait a little longer, honey."

the whole nine yards, but I want to do it our way. And I wanted to give you the picket fence. But that's all, nothing else to resemble the all-American two-point-five kids, one dog, one cat, apple-pie family. I want us just to be us. I want and love you just the way you are."

"Our own world?" she asked.

Smiling, he agreed. "Our own world. By the way," he added, lifting a finger to her lapel again. "I'm not sure I like your new look."

Tasha glanced down at the dull navy. "When I was shopping for it, I wasn't having a good time. But you know, somehow I ended up in the men's department, fingering a Brooks Brothers suit. That's when I decided I had to find you, no matter what. And if I was going to have to go the conservative route, too—"

"It's nothing but outer trappings, Tasha. Didn't you learn anything in Jamaica?"

"I was trying to fit into your world."

He shook his head. "Don't."

"Really?"

"I'd rather fit into yours. In fact," he leaned closer, his lips grazing her ear, "I'd rather see you in nothing at all. You know that farm I bought? We've got forty-seven acres of secluded land, partly wooded, on which we can run around naked any time we want. I haven't seen it yet, but they say there's a perfect spot for a house high on a hill."

Tasha pulled back, feigning surprise. "You mean I can get rid of the suit?"

A house of their own?

about the medicinal quality of herbs and essential oils and I've been thinking I could market them nationwide—"

"Or you could sell them in my shop." Tasha's voice was soft, quiet, as she stepped closer to him.

Andrew reached out and pulled her closer. He threaded his fingers in her hair, tilting her face up to his. "Or I could sell them in your shop," he whispered, his lips dipping dangerously close to hers. "I figure with your knowledge and my sales experience . . ."

He stopped, staring into her eyes. "I've missed you like crazy."

It was warm where their bodies touched. Tasha sighed as they made contact. "I was coming to find you," she said softly. "I was a fool to leave, but I was afraid. Forgive me?"

He nodded. "I was afraid I'd never see you again."

"Did you really quit your job?"

"It was those damned purple ties. The boss didn't like them. I figured clothes were just the outer trappings of our society and what the hell difference did it make if I wore a purple tie instead of black or gray or navy? The day I came to work in blue jeans blew him away."

Fresh tears filled Tasha's eyes and she laughed out loud. She loved him so.

Andrew threaded his fingers into the hair on either side of her head as he searched her eyes. His lips took hers quickly in a short, nibbling kiss. "I want to give you everything you want, Tasha. I want to give you a life together—you, me, kids,